P9-DXT-924

"Mind if I ride with you?"
His dark eyes raked over her.

Their gazes connected in a way that they hadn't before, seeing each other through different eyes, in a new light.

She wrapped her arms around his neck and wiggled onto his lap. "I'd love nothing better," she whispered against his mouth before trailing the tip of her tongue tantalizingly across his lips.

He took her mouth in a long, slow kiss, pulled her closer, pressing her breasts against his chest. Danielle moaned ever so softly, running her fingers through his hair and pulling him deeper into the kiss.

With great reluctance, he pulled back. "Keep this up and we won't be getting anywhere near Mia's house anytime soon."

"That's the point." She gave him a devilish grin. "Mia can wait," she said, her voice thick with growing need. "But I can't."

Books by Donna Hill

Kimani Romance

Love Becomes Her
If I Were Your Woman
After Dark
Sex and Lies
Seduction and Lies

DONNA HILL

began writing novels in 1990. Since then she has had more than forty titles published, including full-length novels and novellas. Two of her novels and one novella were adapted for television. She has won numerous awards for her body of work. She is also the editor of five novels, two of which were nominated for awards. Donna easily moves from romance to erotica, horror, comedy and women's fiction. She is the first recipient of a Trailblazer Award and currently teaches writing at the Frederick Douglass Creative Arts Center. Donna lives in Brooklyn with her family. Visit her Web site at www.donnahill.com.

SEDUCTION AND LIES

DONNA HILL

ESSENCE BESTSELLING AUTHOR

If you purchased this book without a cover you should be aware
that this book is stolen property. It was reported as "unsold and
destroyed" to the publisher, and neither the author nor the
publisher has received any payment for this "stripped book."

This book is dedicated to all my loyal fans.
I hope you enjoy this latest installment in the TLC series.

 KIMANI PRESS™

Recycling programs
for this product may
not exist in your area.

ISBN-13: 978-0-373-86092-0
ISBN-10:   0-373-86092-7

SEDUCTION AND LIES

Copyright © 2008 by Donna Hill

All rights reserved. The reproduction, transmission or utilization
of this work in whole or in part in any form by any electronic, mechanical
or other means, now known or hereafter invented, including xerography,
photocopying and recording, or in any information storage or retrieval
system, is forbidden without written permission. For permission please
contact Kimani Press, Editorial Office, 233 Broadway, New York, NY
10279 U.S.A.

This is a work of fiction. Names, characters, places and incidents are
either the product of the author's imagination or are used fictitiously,
and any resemblance to actual persons, living or dead, business establishments,
events or locales is entirely coincidental.

® and TM are trademarks. Trademarks indicated with ® are registered in
the United States Patent and Trademark Office, the Canadian Trade Marks
Office and/or other countries.

www.kimanipress.com

Printed in U.S.A.

Dear Reader,

Welcome back to The Ladies Cartel! If you missed Book 1, *Sex and Lies*...tsk, tsk, but now is your chance to catch up.

Seduction and Lies brings fashion photographer Danielle Holloway to the front lines. With her best friend and Cartel member Savannah Blake in her first trimester of pregnancy, Danielle has to take over the assignment and get a crash course in Cartel operations in order to take on a major identity-theft operation that is happening in New York City.

Of course, she can't reveal to anyone outside the Cartel what she does "on the side," and that includes keeping her sexy live-in lover Nick Mateo in the dark. That, however, is extremely difficult as they not only live together, they work together as well.

As Danielle works toward solving her case, she must also work on the secrets about her own identity that have always haunted her, and on her inability to commit to the unabashed love of Nick.

I do hope you enjoy this latest episode with the ladies of the Cartel, and for those who enjoyed my PAUSE FOR MEN series, Ann Marie, Stephanie and Elizabeth make cameo appearances.

Steamy sex, secrets and surprises. What more could a romance reader want? LOL.

I had fun, and I hope you will as well. I'd love to hear your thoughts. Feel free to send me an e-mail at writerdoh@aol.com.

Until next time,

Donna

Chapter 1

Danielle Holloway pranced into her kitchen wearing a pink thong adorned along the waistband with tiny rhinestones, and not much else. She pulled open the camel-colored wood cabinet above the sink and took out two plates. Cooking really wasn't her thing, but for Nick she was willing to make the effort—hopefully she wouldn't kill him in the process.

She opened the freezer and took out a box of Aunt Jemima frozen waffles and a box of frozen Jimmy Dean turkey sausage. She was pretty sure she had some syrup around somewhere.

"Need some help?" came the rough-textured voice behind her.

Slowly she turned around, her size-C breasts standing at attention.

Nick's dark blue, almost black, eyes rolled over her from head to toe. Dani watched his throat work up and down as his gaze caressed every inch of her, reminding her quite vividly of the night and half the morning they'd spent together.

What she felt for Nick Mateo scared her—badly. Sometimes when she was around him, she couldn't breathe, her thoughts would get scrambled and her heart would beat so fast she thought she'd faint. She thought about him when she should have been concentrating on a photo shoot or developing film. He made her laugh, and thoughts of being without him made her want to cry. She was in love for the first time in her adult life, and she was scared as hell. And to compound it all, Nick Mateo was white—at least legally. Well, kinda white. His mom was black, his dad Italian. She was half black and half Hispanic, which accounted for her waist-length, raven-black hair and honey-brown complexion. Both of them had to check "other" on all those applications. She had enough cultural issues to deal with on her own—and now his as well.

Nonetheless, together, Nick and Dani made a stunning couple. He, a subtle look-alike for a young Alec Baldwin, dark short hair, a sexy five-o'clock shadow and a body to die for. She, a striking beauty whose face could easily grace the pages of fashion magazines.

He sauntered toward her with a pearl-gray towel wrapped around his narrow hips and slid his muscular arms around her waist. He nuzzled her neck, and Dani's body warmed all over.

"I…was going to fix us something to eat," she said

on a breath, inhaling his cool, clean scent from his recent shower. She tilted her head back to give him better access to that spot that made her weak in the knees.

He held her a little tighter. "I already have something to eat." He nibbled her neck and ran his hands along the curve of her spine. Dani moaned. "God, I can't get enough of you," he groaned. He drew in a long, hot breath and reluctantly stepped back. He looked deep into her eyes, down into her soul. "I'm in love with you—you better know that."

Dani's heart banged in her chest. "Me, too." It was as close as she had come to saying the *L* word.

"I'll settle for that," he said, knowing the emotional struggle Dani was having wrestling with her feelings. Admitting that she could be vulnerable enough to turn her heart and soul over to someone else was something she wasn't ready to handle. He was willing to give her as much time as she needed. He knew what was in her heart. He could see it when she looked at him, when she moaned his name as he made love to her, when she laughed at his stupid jokes and told him about her life and her deepest fears. They had no secrets between them, and that was why he knew this relationship was going to work, whether or not she ever said the *L* word.

Danielle kissed him on the lips, tasting the minty toothpaste. "So are you going to be a help or a hindrance in the kitchen?"

He peeked over her shoulder to see what was on the menu. He turned up his nose. "How 'bout I fix us breakfast?"

A sunshiny smile bloomed across her face. "Sure."

Nick shook his head and chuckled. "You didn't have to give in so quickly, ya know. Let me put on some clothes—pickings are kinda thin in the fridge, if I remember correctly." He kissed her on the tip of her nose, turned and went into the bedroom to get dressed.

"Whataman," she murmured.

Savannah Fields woke up on Sunday morning and barely made it to the bathroom. She was only in her first trimester, and morning sickness was kicking her butt—*day and night*.

"You okay, baby?" Blake called from the other side of the bathroom door.

Savannah splashed cold water on her face, leaned over the sink and drew in long, slow breaths in the hopes of controlling the rocking and rolling going on in her stomach. How could something that would ultimately be so precious make you feel like you wanted to die?

"I'm…fine," she was finally able to say. "Be out in a minute."

Slowly she raised her head and gazed at her reflection in the mirror. The doctor assured her that the morning sickness would stop after three months. She still had one to go. She gripped the side of the sink as another wave of nausea swept through her belly and made her head spin.

Savannah moaned. How was she going to be able to fulfill her latest undercover assignment if she could barely hold her head up? She was going to need help.

Jean Armstrong, the head of The Ladies Cartel—affectionately known as TLC—had called her into the Cartel offices at the brownstone on 135th Street in

Harlem three weeks earlier to congratulate her on the successful completion of her last assignment, which was to uncover a suspected land fraud deal in downtown Brooklyn. What Savannah had uncovered was not only a major scam but also the fact that the development was going to be built on top of an ancient African burial ground. It had been a difficult assignment, and not so much because it was her first but because her husband, Blake, was the contractor on the deal and she was bound by her oath to the Cartel not to reveal what she was doing to anyone—and that included her husband.

Her investigation had also led her to believe that her husband, her soul mate, was not only involved in the unscrupulous land deal but also was having an affair with the woman who was behind it all, millionaire heiress Tristan Montgomery. Savannah needed the help of her two best friends, Danielle Holloway and Mia Turner, to prove otherwise, and they did.

Unfortunately, Savannah had broken a major rule of The Ladies Cartel by involving anyone who was not a sworn member. Fortunately for her, it had turned out well, and Jean reminded her how lucky she was when she gave her this latest assignment.

Savannah flushed the toilet and rinsed out her mouth. At least her head had stopped spinning.

One thing she knew for certain was that she was going to have to break some more rules if she was to get the next job accomplished. She could certainly use the skills of the Cartel members, but she knew she could trust Dani and Mia more than any other two people on earth.

Blake knocked on the door. "Savannah, are you okay?"

"Coming." Gingerly she made her way to the door and opened it.

Blake was standing on the other side with a distraught look on his ruggedly handsome face. She smiled wanly.

He put his arm around her shoulder. "Can I get you anything?"

"Yeah, a time machine. Speed this process up by about seven months."

Blake grinned and kissed the top of her head, and led her back to the bed. "If I could, you know I would, baby."

She waved off the bed. "I think I need to move around. I want to meet the girls for a late lunch."

"You sure you're up to it?"

She nodded. "Yeah, some ginger ale and a few crackers, and I'll be good as new." She left his embrace and went into the kitchen. Moments later she could hear the blare and roar of a basketball game coming from the living-room television set.

Must be Sunday, she mused, smiling as she popped open a can of ice-cold ginger ale and took a long, refreshing swallow. Sunday was game day in the Fields' household. Blake carved out his position on the couch and watched games all day long, nonstop, even if they were on videotape, which gave Savannah the perfect opportunity to hang out with the girls. And today they needed an emergency meeting.

While Nick was at the local grocer, Dani took a quick shower and straightened up the bedroom. As she sat on the edge of the bed, applying the Victoria's Secret brand of lotion that Nick loved, her phone rang.

She turned behind her, reached across the bed and picked up the phone from the nightstand. Lying on her stomach, she answered.

"Hello?"

"Hey, Dani, it's me, Savannah."

"Hey, girl, how ya feeling?"

"Don't ask."

"You're a better woman than me."

"Listen, I was hoping the three of us could get together this afternoon."

"Hmm, what time? Me and Nick were getting ready to fix something to eat."

"You mean, Nick is fixing something to eat."

Dani giggled. "Don't hate."

"How about four at The Shop? Maybe by then my stomach will have settled down to a quiet roar."

The digital clock on the nightstand illuminated eleven.

"Sounds good. Did you call Mia?"

"No, not yet. Would you mind? It's going to take me a while to get myself together as it is, and I don't need Mia slowing me down by needing all the details of a simple late lunch."

The friends laughed. Of the trio, Mia Turner was the organizer—to a fault. As head of her own events management business, she was a stickler for planning each and every move. Although it was an outrageously annoying habit, her obsession with order and detail always ultimately paid off.

"Sure. I'll do that as soon as we finish. What's up, anyway? Just need to get out?"

"Actually it's a little more than that." She lowered her

voice and got off the side of the bed to make sure Blake was still parked securely in front of the television. She closed the bedroom door. "I have another assignment, and I need yours and Mia's help."

Mia Turner had been up since daybreak. She fixed a spectacular breakfast for her and Steve—homemade Belgian waffles; egg-white omelets filled with mushrooms, tomatoes, green peppers and cheddar cheese; fresh orange juice and an incredible Turkish coffee that she'd received from one of her corporate clients as a thank-you gift.

Of the trio it had always been efficient Mia who hadn't had a man in her life. Savannah had Blake and before Danielle finally starting playing house with Nick, she always had men to keep her warm and well tuned.

Mia had always known about Steve Long: she'd seen him from a distance from time to time, since he and Savannah's husband, Blake, were tight buddies and business partners. But they'd never spent any time together, and it had never occurred to Mia to do so. It wasn't until she'd planned a get-together, with Steve being an invited guest, that they both realized what they'd been missing. They'd been an item ever since, and Mia couldn't have been happier.

Steve left shortly after breakfast for a game of tennis, and Mia decided to get a jump start on the week. She went into her immaculate office, where not a paper clip was out of place, and settled down for a few hours of planning. She had several corporate clients that were planning major conferences as well as restaurant locations that she needed to set up for more intimate meetings.

She turned on her seventeen-inch flat-screen computer and quickly clicked on her color-coded spreadsheet program; then she opened up another program window, this one with a grid of Manhattan.

Just as she started plugging in information, her phone rang. It was Dani.

"Hey, girl, what's up?" Mia kept her attention on the screen while she talked to Dani on speaker.

"I hate that damned speakerphone! Makes me sound like I'm underwater."

"Oh, don't be silly."

"Can you please just stop doing what you're doing and pay attention to me for a minute?"

"You know, you sound like a whiny five-year-old," Mia said, taking the call off speaker. "Better now?"

"Much," Dani said with a huff.

"So what is it? You're breaking my flow."

"Savannah just called. She wants us to get together around four at The Shop."

Mia frowned. That was not on her agenda for the day. She'd have to rearrange things to make that happen. If there was one thing that worked Mia's nerves more than anything, it was surprises that knocked off her schedule and her plans.

"Well, okay. I'll have to shift around a few things. Why today? Did she say what it was about? Our get-togethers are always planned in advance…"

"Dang, Mia. This *is* the best advance notice we can

give. Five damned hours. Now do whatever it is that you do to get yourself in gear, and we'll see you there at four."

Mia huffed with indignation. "You don't have to be nasty… I was just saying…"

She almost sounded hurt, Dani thought. "I'm sorry. Didn't mean to snap. You know my mouth sometimes. Anyway, Savannah said it was important." She paused. "She needs our help."

Mia knew exactly what that meant.

Chapter 2

For four o'clock on a Sunday, The Shop, located in the West Village, was pretty crowded. The hum of conversation interspersed with bits of laughter floated over the pulse of some nondescript listening music.

Although she'd complained about the disruption in her day, Mia was, of course, the first to arrive and had secured their favorite booth in the back. She was sipping on a mimosa when Dani walked in looking like a supermodel, followed moments later by Savannah, whose petite frame was getting plumper by the day.

"Movin' kinda slow there, sis," Dani teased, as Savannah lowered herself into the seat next to Mia.

Savannah put her purse on her lap and took off her sunglasses, setting them on the table. "Don't make fun. It ain't funny," she grumbled over a half smile.

Mia put her arm around Savannah's shoulder and pulled her in for a short hug. "At least you look cute."

That much was true. Much like Danielle, Savannah loved to dress, and being pregnant only upped the ante. She was determined that the worse she felt, the better she would look. No expense was spared when it came to her wardrobe.

Today, she wore a bolero sweater, cuffed at the elbow, in a sea-moss green that sparkled in the sunlight, over an empire shirt in the same color, with tight accordion pleats that fell just to the waistband of her designer jeans, and a pair of emerald-green ankle boots in butter-soft suede.

"Thanks. And thanks for coming."

"No problem," the duo murmured.

Dani flipped open a menu. "So whatsup?"

Savannah leaned forward. Dani and Mia drew closer.

"I got another assignment."

"We figured as much," Dani said. "So how can we help?"

"I got major grief from Jean about pulling you two in the last time around. But because everything turned out so well, she sort of gave me a pass to 'use my resources.' Anyway, I've been feeling so crappy I know I can't handle this alone at all."

"The suspense is killing me already. What is it?" Dani asked.

"Well, it's identity theft."

"Whoa." Mia reared back, then lowered her voice. "For real? Like the kind of identity theft that's been on the news lately?"

Savannah nodded. "Apparently there is a major ring operating right here in New York."

Dani leaned in. "Why aren't the cops or the FBI or somebody handling this?"

"They are. But it goes a little deeper than that. This thing is extremely sensitive due to the nature of the people involved, so Jean was called in by a friend of hers in the Bureau."

"This is pretty major," Mia said.

"There's more." Savannah folded her hands. "This is where it gets kind of James Bond-y. There are some folks that have come to Jean…on a personal level. People who can't go to the police or the FBI and who are in the same boat." She looked from one friend to the other, making sure they got her meaning. Their eyes brightened in understanding.

"Illegals?" Dani asked.

"No. Just folks who can't be scrutinized by the authorities. They can't risk this showing up in the media."

Mia flopped back against the leather seat. "How much time do you have?"

"A few weeks. A month at best."

"That's going to be a problem on my end. I'm out of town for the next two weeks setting up several conventions, one in Atlanta the other in D.C. I leave tomorrow afternoon. Of course I'll do what I can—any contacts and resources that I can provide…"

"Count me in," Dani said. "Do you think I'll get to use a gun this time?" Her eyes sparkled with hope.

Both Savannah and Mia looked at her and shook their heads.

"I would hope not," Savannah said.

Dani sucked her teeth in disappointment. "Figures."

"However, this time I'm not taking any chances. This is major and we can't afford to screw this up." She zeroed in on Danielle. "I'm going to make sure I have clearance to bring you in. You're going to have to meet Jean."

A big grin dashed across Danielle's mocha-colored face. "The head chick in charge! Well, all righty then. That's what I'm talking about."

"What about me?" Mia whined.

"Since you won't be directly involved, I don't think it's necessary."

"Damn." She finished off her drink and slunk down in her seat, pouting.

The waitress finally came over. "Sorry, ladies. It's crazy busy. Can I get you anything?"

They flipped open their menus and one by one gave their orders.

"Now that we have that out of the way, how have you both been doing?" Savannah asked, sipping a glass of water.

"I finally know what always keeps a smile on the two of your faces," Mia said.

"Oh, really?" Dani said with a raised brow. "And what might that be?"

"Having a fine, sexy man to wake up to every morning." She flashed a wicked grin and a wink.

Savannah and Dani laughed.

"So you've discovered the secret of sublime happiness," Savannah said.

Mia bobbed her head. "Yes, chile," she said, emphasizing each word. "Steven is absolutely a dream come true. And to think we've known each other for years and never took it further than hello." She looked off wistfully. "It's just so wonderful. I mean, I've never really had anyone that made me feel good all…the…time. Know what I mean?" She looked from one to the other.

Well, there was someone once, but she'd never told her friends about him then and with good reason. And with everything going so right in her life with Steven there was no point in bringing it up now. It was old news and best that it stay buried in the past.

"I know exactly what you mean," Dani offered. "And you know me, Ms. Love 'em and Leave 'em. I think I've been whipped, my sistahs."

Savannah and Mia applauded.

"We never thought we'd see the day," Savannah said.

"Me, either. Nick has totally taken me by surprise. It's like those romance novels where the heroine gets swept off her feet and lands flat on her back, ready and raring to go," she added in her typical ribald fashion.

The trio broke up laughing.

"Some days," Savannah offered, "it's still hard for me to believe that me and Blake are still so crazy in love and still hungry for each other."

"Even with the loaf in the oven?" Dani asked.

Savannah's eyes widened. "Girl, it's even worse. When I'm not sick, I'm horny as hell! Can't wait for the man to get home from work! Hormones are in overdrive or something. And Blake, Lawd, he never felt so good!"

Dani started fanning herself and Mia quickly followed suit.

Their meals arrived, and they continued swapping stories of their scorching love lives.

* * *

Outside the restaurant, the three women hugged.

"Have a safe trip, Mia," Savannah said. "And I'll be in touch if I can use your help."

"Yeah, take care, sis." Dani kissed her cheek. "What is Steven going to do while you're gone?"

"Miss me." She rocked her head to the side. "I intend to wear the brother out before I leave. Make sure it holds him over until I get back."

"Now that's gangsta," Dani teased.

"See you guys in two weeks." Mia waved as she headed down the street to where her car was parked.

Savannah turned to face Danielle. "Let me know when you have some free time. I'm going to call Jean in the morning and try to set up a meeting as soon as possible."

"You know me. I'm my own boss. My schedule is pretty light this week with photo shoots. I have a couple of location shots, but that's it."

"Great. So as soon as I get it set up, I will give you a call."

"Sounds good."

"Thanks, Dani, I really appreciate this."

"Hey, that's what superspy friends are for, right?" she teased.

"Yeah, exactly."

When Danielle returned to her apartment, it was empty. She was surprised that Nick wasn't there. He hadn't mentioned he was going out.

She tossed her purse on the table in the hall and deposited her keys in the glass bowl right next to it before heading to the kitchen for an ice-cold beer.

She took her beer and went to the so-called second bedroom, which served as her office/darkroom. There should be a law against false advertising, she thought, as she flipped on the light. When she'd read the ad for the "spacious two-bedroom apartment" some five years ago, she was expecting spacious. Well, the "second bedroom" was about eight feet long and five feet wide. The only person who could sleep in there was a midget. If you put a full-size bed in the room you'd have to walk over it to get in and out! So she'd converted it to a tiny office space with a flat-screen computer, a small desk and her photography equipment, which was stored in the closet. With a few shelves mounted on the wall, it actually became a functional space.

Danielle had a photo shoot scheduled for the following morning and wanted to go over the shot schedule. There were five models involved in the shoot for a new designer who was launching a line for the fall. They were going to set up in the Central Park Zoo so that the caged animals could serve as a backdrop.

The weather for the next day was set to be in the high seventies, which would make for a very uncomfortable day for the models and the crew.

She went down her list of supplies for the day, making sure to include two cases of water and an ice cooler.

The front door opened and shut, and the sound of male voices filled the front room.

Danielle pushed her papers aside and went to the front room.

"Hey, hon," Danielle greeted Nick, as she strolled up to him in the living room and kissed him lightly on the lips. She turned to their guest. "Bernard…"

"Good to see you again, Danielle."

She'd met Bernard Hassell several weeks earlier at a get-together at Mia's house. Bernard was a dead ringer for Billy Dee Williams and the current love interest of Claudia, Savannah's mother.

"You, too, Bernard." Her brow wrinkled ever so slightly. "Where did you two hook up?"

"At the gym," Nick said. "Well, as I was going to the gym. Bernard was walking by on his way to this new spot, Pause for Men. He invited me to join him." Nick grinned. "The place is fabulous. Full spa, exercise rooms, saunas—the works—and a health-food cafe."

Bernard hooked his thumb over his shoulder toward Nick. "I think Pause just got a new member." He chuckled lightly.

Dani eyed Bernard. "Wow, no wonder you stay in such great shape," she teased.

Bernard grinned and made a slight bow. "I'll take that as a compliment."

"Can I offer you something to drink?" she asked, moving toward the kitchen.

"We were gonna grab a couple of beers and catch the end of the game," Nick said, pecking her cheek. "How was the afternoon with the girls?"

"Fine," she answered absentmindedly, trying to wrap her mind around the odd matchup of her man with one old enough to be his dad. "Well, I'll leave you boys to your games. Good to see you again, Bernard," she said before returning to her office.

Once inside, she closed the door behind her and dialed Mia on her cell.

"Hey, Dani, whatsup?"

Danielle cut a quick glance toward the closed door, then spoke in a harsh whisper. "Guess who's here?"

"What? Why are you whispering?"

"Put your damned glasses on so you can hear me!"

"Not funny. Abuse I don't need," Mia said haughtily. "Now, speak up."

Danielle blew out an exasperated breath. "Bernard is here."

"Who?"

"Bernard! Claudia's Bernard."

"Savannah's mom, Claudia?"

"Yes!" she hissed.

"Why? Did something happen to Claudia?"

"No. He's hanging out with Nick, of all things. They met at some spa." She shook her head in bewilderment.

"Soooo…the problem is…?"

"Don't you think it's odd? I mean, Bernard is…older."

Mia laughed. "Guys aren't like women, D. They bond over all sorts of stuff, sports, video games. Age isn't an issue with them."

"Hmm, I guess…"

"Besides, didn't you say Nick lost his dad when he was a teen?"

"Yes."

"Maybe Bernie's like a substitute or something."

"You're probably right. I'm making something out of nothing."

"Bet they're watching a game and drinking beer."

Danielle giggled. "Exactly."

"See what I mean? Anyway, relax. I need to pack. And don't forget if you and Savannah need my help…"

"I know, sis. Thanks."

"Good luck. I mean that."

"Thanks. Safe travels."

"Safe spying."

That was what she should be focused on, Danielle reasoned as she disconnected the call—working her first undercover assignment.

She couldn't wait to meet Jean.

The sounds of male laughter drifted into the bedroom. Even with Mia's wise words about male bonding, she still couldn't shake her misgivings about Bernard. It was nothing that she could actually put her finger on. He was nice enough and obviously Claudia cared about him. But he simply seemed too good to be true: handsome, smooth talking, well put-together for a man of his age, and he seemed to have plenty of time on his hands. What did he do for a living? How could he afford a fancy spa like the one they were talking about, and where did he come from, anyway? She was probably overanalyzing, seeing ghosts in the closet when there weren't any. She pushed her wayward thoughts about Bernard Hassell to the back of her mind, at least for the time being. She had more pressing matters to concentrate on. Her first assignment. She grinned with anticipation.

Chapter 3

It was three nerve-racking days before Savannah heard from Jean with a date for the meeting.

"Do I look okay?" Danielle asked for the tenth time in as many minutes as they drove to the Cartel brownstone.

"Dani, I swear, if you ask me just one more time…"

"I want to make a good impression."

"You'll be fine. And when have you not made a good impression?" She paused, frowned slightly. "Well, there was that time in the restaurant in Chelsea when your name wasn't on the reservation list, and the time you got into a shouting match with that model's agent during a photo shoot, and the time…"

Danielle held up her hand. "All right, all right! I'll behave. I get it." She huffed and folded her arms.

"What I'm trying to say, sweetie, is you always *look*

fabulous, but you simply have to keep your temper in check and be, uh, more diplomatic."

Of the trio, Danielle was notorious for flying off the handle at the drop of a hat, and it didn't take much for her to feel slighted. But most of her flare-ups occurred when she felt one of her friends was being mistreated or the people she expected to fall in line, such as staff, support people and…well, the general public, didn't live up to what *she* expected of them. But if you ever wanted anyone in the trenches with you, it was definitely Danielle. She would go down swinging and still look incredible.

"I want to make a good impression," Danielle finally said, looking uncharacteristically uncertain. She tugged on her bottom lip with her teeth.

"You'll be fine." Savannah reached across the gears and squeezed Danielle's hand. "I promise."

Danielle looked into Savannah's eyes and saw the confidence there. She drew in a long breath. "Thanks."

"Here we are."

Danielle peeked out the window at the very stately four-story brownstone, which looked like all the other well-taken-care-of homes on the restored block. "This is it?"

Savannah chuckled. "What did you expect? The Batcave?" She unfastened her seat belt and got out. "Come on."

Danielle followed Savannah to the ground-floor entrance of the house.

"See that house across the street?" Savannah said, lifting her chin toward the house.

"You mean, where that F-I-N-E man is going in followed by another one?"

"Yes, it's a day spa for men."

"Get out."

"Yep, run by four women, best friends."

"What? Wait a minute. Is it called Pause for Men?"

"Yeah, why?" She pressed the bell. A chime echoed gently in the background.

"Uh, nothing. I think I heard about it somewhere." That sounded like the same spa that Bernard had taken Nick to, she thought. She'd have to make sure, and if it was, hopefully she wouldn't have to come to headquarters too often. That could get pretty sticky. And she certainly wasn't about to mention anything to Savannah to give her or Jean a reason not to give her this assignment.

The door opened. Savannah recognized Margaret, the woman the Cartel had honored the previous month for having been responsible for shutting down a senior retirement home in Brooklyn that had been abusing the seniors.

"Hi. We're here to see Jean."

"Come in. Come in. Good to see you again, Savannah," the middle-aged Cartel member said with a warm smile. Tiny laugh lines fanned out from the corners of her blue eyes.

"Margaret, this is Danielle Holloway."

Margaret stared at her for a long moment then turned to Savannah. "Looks like she has what it takes." She winked. "It's all in the eyes. Make yourselves comfortable a moment. I'll let Jean know you're here."

"Thanks, Margaret," Savannah said with a light laugh.

"That was weird," Danielle said under her breath.
"Did you see how she looked at me?"

Savannah waved her hand in dismissal. "That's one
of the top agents. She's been with the Cartel since the
beginning, and she's Jean's right hand. Definitely
someone you want on your side, and if she says you've
got what it takes, then you've got it."

"If you say so," Danielle murmured, glancing up at
the twelve-foot ceiling and the incredible crystal chan-
delier that looked like something out of a holiday movie.
She slowly strolled around the massive room and took
in the decor.

Antique furnishings dotted the enormous room. Sunshine spilled across the sparkling parquet floors from
eight-foot-long windows treated with sheer white curtains billowing ever so gently from the light breeze. An
oak mantle with a massive fireplace was the center-
piece of the room, reminiscent of the great party days
of old Harlem.

Margaret appeared in the doorway as silently as she'd
left. "Jean is ready for you," she said.

She led them upstairs, turned right at the top of the
landing and walked down a long hallway that was lined
on either side with photographs of Cartel members. Danielle caught a glimpse of Savannah's mother, Claudia, and
just before Margaret tapped on the partially opened door,
Danielle saw a picture of a smiling Savannah.

*Wow, it's like going to the White House or some-
where prestigious and seeing the rows of presidents
hanging on the walls,* she thought, then she wondered
if her picture would wind up there one day.

Margaret opened the door, stepped aside and let Savannah and Danielle pass. "Good luck," she whispered to Danielle before closing the door behind her.

The room was dimly lit by an antique lamp on a desk behind which Jean sat. Outdoor sunshine was blocked by the heavy brocade drapes, in sharp contrast to the floor below.

"Ladies." Jean took off her pink-framed glasses and stood. "Thank you for coming. Please have a seat." Her radiant red hair fell in soft waves around her delicate face to brush her shoulders.

Danielle noticed that her skin was almost translucent as a trickle of perspiration shimmied down the center of her own spine even though the air-conditioning was running at optimum level. She took a seat opposite Jean and next to Savannah. She crossed her ankles and drew in a long, calming breath, then put on her best smile.

"How are you feeling these days, Savannah?"

Savannah gently patted her barely noticeable baby bump. "If I can get past these first three months, I just might survive."

Jean offered a lukewarm smile. "Children." Her right brow flicked reflexively. "They never factored into my life—always busy traveling, getting from one assignment to the next." She sighed. "Now it's too late."

"I'm sorry," Savannah offered.

"Oh, don't be," she said with a wave of her hand. "I'd make a terrible mother. I don't have a nurturing bone in my body." She turned her attention to Danielle. "Ms. Holloway." She said it in such a way that it hung in the air, more like an accusation than a greeting.

Danielle swallowed and offered a tight-lipped smile, feeling as if she'd been caught with her top off in the boys' locker room with the captain of the basketball team. "It's good to meet you."

"I'm sure that Savannah told you this is completely against protocol. This is not how we recruit members." She tossed Savannah a sharp look, and Savannah adjusted her behind in her seat. "However, because Savannah did such an excellent job on her first assignment and was recruited by her mother, whom I hold in the highest regard…" She drew in a breath, then on the exhale said, "I've decided after much deliberation and consultation, to consider your admittance."

Danielle felt her lungs fill with air and realized that she'd been holding her breath. She almost broke out in laughter, she was so relieved.

"However, you have no skills. You haven't been trained. Ideally I should be using one of our more seasoned members, but I wanted Savannah for this job. Obviously she can't handle it now, and because you and Mia Turner were so integral to resolving the land fraud deal, I think that you would be a perfect substitute."

"Thank you." I *think*.

"You're going to have to take a crash course. We don't have much time to get you up to speed. You will need to master in two weeks what would normally take two to three months. If I'm satisfied with your progress at the end of the training, you'll get your kit and be briefed on the details of the assignment."

* * *

"Is she always like that?" Danielle asked once they were safely inside Savannah's car.

Savannah grinned. "Like what?"

"So…distant, no-nonsense and…cold." She fastened her seat belt.

"In her position, I think you have to be. She has a lot of responsibility."

"You think she has a man in her life?"

"You would ask something like that," she said, laughing. "Why?"

"Just figured if she had a man, it would loosen the lines around her mouth."

Savannah cracked up. "Girl, you are terrible."

"Just honest. Anyway," she continued as Savannah pulled off, "what does this training entail?"

"Well…"

It was nearly nine by the time Danielle got home. She'd told Nick that she was going with Savannah after work to look at cribs.

"Hey, babe," Nick said from the archway of the kitchen. He brushed a damp lock of hair away from his forehead and stepped out, a towel wrapped around his waist. His torso was a series of hard ripples, his slightly tanned skin glistening with water where the towel had missed. His eyes sparkled and crinkled at the corners when he smiled, which was often.

Danielle's heart sputtered in her chest, and that butterfly feeling in the center of her stomach went on a rampage. Just looking at Nick and having him look at her with such love and lust in his eyes made her weak all over.

She tossed her bag on the counter and slowly approached him. He leaned against the frame of the door. She stood right in front of him, barely a breath away, and pressed the palms of her hands against his chest.

Nick lowered his head, brushed her fluttering eyelids with his lips.

Danielle felt the heat tap out a rhythm between her thighs.

Nick snaked an arm around her waist, his other hand cupped the back of her head. His mouth dragged down her upturned face, planting kisses until he reached her lips; then he took her mouth in movie close-up fashion, slow, soft and sure.

Danielle's body vibrated. She sighed into his mouth as his tongue played with hers.

Nick pulled her tightly against him. Dani groaned, feeling the bulge of his erection press firmly against her stomach.

He lifted his mouth from Danielle's. Her eyes remained slightly parted, then fluttered open. Nick's lips curved upward.

"And how was your day?" he teased, stroking her back.

Danielle pressed her head against his chest. "It just got better, but I need to get settled."

"No problem. I fixed dinner. Come on out when you're ready."

She tilted her head back, looked into his inky dark eyes and lost herself in the light that danced in their depths.

"I…I'm crazy about you," she whispered over the sudden tightness in her throat.

For a nanosecond she caught the flash of disappointment that passed across his gorgeous face and dimmed his eyes. Then it was gone, and that half smile that always made her melt was in place.

"I know." His gaze locked with hers, seeing beyond her words.

Danielle tugged in a breath. "I'll be out in a few." She picked up her purse from the hall table and walked toward their bedroom. She plopped down on the side of bed and took off her shoes.

A sense of exhilaration rippled through her. She had her first assignment—well, almost—and she couldn't wait to get started with her training. Two weeks, humph, she could handle it. Piece of cake.

She got up from the bed and began to take off her clothes. Walking into the bathroom and turning on the shower, she wondered how she was going to handle Nick, especially if he was going to the spa right across the street. Geez, how freaky was that?

Not only did she and Nick live together, but they also worked together as fashion photographers. Their days were busy, often grueling yet at the same time exciting. They loved what they did and were as passionate about their work as they were about each other. The adrenaline rush that they felt all day while shooting those perfect shots, getting the lighting just right to frame the model, spilled over into the bedroom, where they strove for the perfection that would run them all day as they watched the other work—Nick getting

turned on watching Danielle style the set, then get behind the lens to capture the moment, or Dani as she
looked on while Nick, now behind the camera, coaxed
and cooed at the models to bring out that special something that would pop on film.

Maybe that was what made their lovemaking so
intense, so passionate and earth-shaking, Danielle
thought, as she stepped under the rush of water. The need
that built up between them all day exploded at night.

She knew their relationship was more than great sex.
There were feelings involved. Nick was in love with her.
She knew it, she felt it, he admitted it.

She also knew that she had deep feelings for Nick. She
felt it deep in her soul. It was probably love—something
she admitted hesitantly to Savannah and Mia but never
to Nick. She couldn't. If she did, it would become real—
and if it was real, it could hurt her and she could lose
again.

Danielle lathered her body with her favorite mango
body wash, running her hands over her smooth skin.
They settled for a moment over her flat stomach.

Life once bloomed there. Once. Not even Savannah
or Mia knew. She never spoke about it. Too painful.
Because, of course, if she said it out loud, it would be
real and that devastating reality she wouldn't deal with.

So she kept that dark part of her life buried so deep
beneath the surface that she hardly thought about it,
especially because she could cover it all up with beauty,
excitement, work—and now Nick Mateo.

Danielle stepped out of the shower stall and wrapped
herself in a thick, pearl-gray towel. Before leaving, she

caught a glimpse of herself in the foggy mirror. The ethereal image evoked a sense of illusion—something or someone being there but not quite. That was her. That was her life.

She opened the door and the cool rush of air blew in, dissolving the steam. Her image cleared. The hazy edges evaporated. There she stood, the way the world saw and knew her. She looked away.

"You and Savannah find a crib?" Nick asked before he lifted a forkful of penne pasta swathed in primavera sauce to his mouth.

"Crib?" For a moment, Danielle had no clue what he was talking about.

"Yeah, you said you two were going crib shopping."

"Oh." She laughed, hoping to cover her gaff. "Yes, uh, we looked around. There were a couple that she really liked." She kept her gaze focused on her mixed-green salad.

Nick angled his head a bit to the right. "Are you okay? You seem out of it since you got home."

She forced herself to look at him, and her heart hammered in her chest as the lie flowed smoothly from her lips. She shrugged, then reached across the small table and covered his hand. "You know the kind of day we had, and then all that walking around from store to store this evening. I don't know how Savannah does it, but I'm beat. That's all."

Nick stared at her a moment.

"For real," she insisted with a smile.

"Okay." He paused. "If something was wrong, you'd tell me, right?"

"Of course."

It was the first lie and, like scalding water it burned her tongue, and she knew it was only the first of many.

"Are you all set for your shoot tomorrow?" she asked, switching to a neutral topic.

"Yeah." He dipped his bread in the sauce and took a bite. "I'm going to the site early to check on the final details."

"If I can finish in time with my meeting with Michael Preston, I'll stop by. I'm determined to get the account to photograph the ads for his new line."

Nick chuckled. "I love when you get that little bass in your voice and that kick-ass look in your eye."

"Very funny," she said, failing at sounding offended.

"It's one of the things I love about you, Dani, that fierce determination, knowing what you want and going after it."

Her gaze dragged over the planes and valleys of his face. That determination that he spoke of was instilled in her as a child growing up in a mixed-heritage household, filling out countless applications and checking "other" for ethnicity, never wanting to negate one parent's heritage for the other and living a life walking that fine line. All of that made her determined to be somebody on her own, independent of tags and labels.

Often she believed that stubborn streak of independence kept her from allowing anyone to get too close, beneath the surface, only to discover that she was no more than a confused girl who was searching for her identity.

She reached over and with the tip of her finger wiped a spot of sauce from the corner of Nick's mouth.

He took her hand and kissed her fingertips, and she silently hoped that when the investigation was all over he would still want to hold her hand.

Chapter 4

If she could land the Michael Preston account, it would take her business to the next level, Danielle thought, as she entered the building on Seventh Avenue—also known as Fashion Avenue. And she was dressed for the part. Her ebony hair flowed in gentle waves around her face. Her five-foot nine-inch frame was the perfect showpiece for the body-hugging, sleeveless, black cotton T-shirt, covered with a belted, hip-length jacket in a riot of orange, gold and muted green, over skinny black jeans that hugged her hips and defined her long legs.

Danielle gripped the handle of her oversize black leather portfolio and stabbed the button for the elevator. Impatiently she tapped her foot, encased in black alligator sling backs with three-inch heels. The finishing touch was her Sean John designer shades, which gave her a hint of mystery. More times than she could count, she'd been mistaken for the songstress Alicia Keys, and although she'd had several opportunities to profit from the mistake, she never had.

The elevator bell dinged and the stainless steel doors soundlessly slid open. She stepped on with two other riders.

Preston's offices were on the thirty-fifth floor of the glass and steel tower. She watched the numbers light up as they ascended.

"Love that jacket," the woman standing next to her said.

Danielle turned. "Thanks."

"Anyone ever tell you look like Alicia Keys?"

Danielle gave a slight smile. "Every now and then."

The woman reached into her purse and pulled out a business card. "If you're ever interested in modeling work, give me a call. I do a whole thing with celebrity look-alikes."

Danielle took the card just as the doors opened on her floor. "Thanks." She stepped off.

"Call me. I'd love to work with you."

Danielle took a quick look at the woman before the doors closed. She walked away, shaking her head in amusement, and stuck the card in her jacket pocket.

She strode down the corridor toward the glass doors with the Michael Preston logo on them. She drew in a breath and pressed the buzzer.

"Yes?" came the voice through the intercom from the fashionista sitting at the desk on the other side of the glass door.

"Danielle Holloway to see Mr. Preston."

The lock buzzed and the door slowly swooshed inward. She entered a space that could only be described as classy. Sleek elegance in simple black and white. Bursting blooms of exotic plants showcased in glass bowls sat majestically on low tables. The stark white walls were adorned with near life-size photographs of models wearing Michael's creations. The frames matched the walls so perfectly that the images seemed to float. It was a powerful optical illusion.

A stunning young woman who couldn't have been more than twenty greeted her. She was pencil thin with startling blue eyes and a mane of strawberry-blond hair that fell straight as a board down the center of her back, held away from her heart-shaped face with a tortoiseshell headband.

"Good morning." She stuck out her hand, which Danielle shook. Her thin lips tinged in dramatic fuchsia widened to reveal a brilliantly perfect smile. "My name is Tasha, Michael's assistant. If you'll follow me, we can get started."

We?

Danielle followed Tasha and the scent of patchouli that wafted around her down a short carpeted hallway, turning right along another that was three times the length of the first. Behind either side of the glass walls, designers were busy at work, their creations in various stages of construction.

Tasha led her to the end of the hallway and opened a heavy inlaid wooden door with Conference Room etched in gold on the front. She stepped aside to let Danielle enter.

Danielle expected to see Michael sitting behind a desk, but he wasn't.

"Please have a seat, I'm eager to see some of your work."

Trying not to show her confusion, which bordered on annoyance, Danielle laid her portfolio on a table that could easily seat twenty, and she unzipped it.

"Uh, is Mr. Preston going to be joining us?"

Tasha gave a little laugh. "Michael is out of town. But not to worry. If I like what I see, he likes what I see."

Danielle blew out a silent breath. *This chick wasn't old enough to know the difference between commercial photography and Photoshop.*

"Actually, I'm a fan of yours," Tasha said, as she sat down and began reviewing Danielle's work.

"Really?" The knot in her stomach loosened.

"I've studied your work at Parsons and The New School for Design in my advertising and marketing classes."

Her brows rose in surprise. "I had no idea."

"You have a very distinct style, Ms. Holloway. I could pick your shots out from a crowd any day."

"I hope that's a good thing."

There was that little laugh again. "I think so."

Tasha closed the book before she was even halfway finished. Not a good sign, Danielle thought.

"I'd like to take you on a tour of the design floor—get your impressions—and then we can wrap up in my office."

A little more than an hour and a half later, Danielle was sitting behind the wheel of her Navigator with a retainer check in her hand for ten thousand dollars.

Her head was still spinning. She'd actually landed the account. She was to be the official photographer for the Michael Preston fall collection.

Her photographs would be on his Web site, in his catalogs and all of his promotional material. They'd wind up in every fashion magazine across the country and in Europe.

She didn't even care why they needed a new photographer. All she knew was that she had finally taken her business to the next level.

This called for some serious celebrating. Under normal circumstances Mia would offer to whip up one of her fabulous meals at her house, since she was the only one of the trio who could really cook. But because she was out of town, Danielle and Nick would have to go out.

She reached for her cell phone to call Nick and give him the good news when the phone chirped in her hand, indicating she had a message waiting. She dialed into her voice mail.

It was Savannah. Danielle's training was to start tonight. She was to come to the TLC headquarters at eight.

Well, that put a wrinkle in things, Danielle thought as she put the SUV in gear and drove off.

Chapter 5

Danielle pulled up to the photo shoot site in midtown Manhattan. As usual, the area had its curious onlookers, but for the most part New Yorkers, who are used to seeing just about anything and everybody, pretty much took a peek and went on their way.

She tossed her parking permit on her dashboard, grabbed her equipment from the passenger seat and hopped out. She ducked under the tape that separated the set from the pedestrians and weaved in and out of the crew until she reached Nick's side.

"How's it going?" she whispered in his ear, causing him to jump in surprise.

Nick turned to her, a smile blooming on his face. He leaned down for a quick kiss. "You made it. Things are cool here. The usual drama. Let's take ten," he shouted.

"So tell me what happened." He slid his arm around her waist and ushered her away from the crowd.

"Wellll." She dragged the word out. "I got it!" She jumped up and down doing a happy dance.

Nick swept her up in his arms and spun her around, drawing the wide-eyed stares of passersby. "Oh, baby— I'm so happy for you!" He kissed her lips.

"Happy for *us*. This is a package deal. It's you and me babe. And I have a ten-thousand-dollar check to prove it."

"Whoa, this is definitely cause for celebration." He pulled her close. "What do you want to do? You name it."

Her heart began to pound. "Well, how about we, uh, plan something for the weekend. Just the two of us."

He gave a slight shrug. "Sure. I didn't think you would want to wait that long."

"We have a crazy week ahead of us and it will be the perfect way to end it." She stroked his jaw.

"Whatever you want," he said halfheartedly.

"Good." She pecked him on the lips. "Now bring me up to speed with the shoot," she said, smoothly switching into business mode.

Danielle followed Nick back over to the set, half listening to him as she tried to think of an excuse for why she would be away for the evening.

"So what are you going to tell him?" Savannah asked.

Danielle turned her back to the people on the set and cradled her phone a bit closer. "I have no idea. Any suggestions? What did you tell Blake during your training?"

"For one thing, Blake and I didn't work together, and he was so accustomed to me working overtime at the law firm that I never really had to come up with an explanation."

"Great," she said with a sigh. "I've already used the shopping-for-cribs excuse."

"Dani!" one of her crew members called out.

She turned in the direction of the voice.

"We need you over here."

"Be right there," she shouted over the noise of traffic. "Gotta go," she said to Savannah. "If you think of anything, call me."

"Will do."

Danielle disconnected the call, stuck her BlackBerry in the case on her hip and joined her team.

The photo shoot was an ad campaign for Lincoln Center's fall season. The bevy of models were attired in gorgeous evening gowns from the Vera Wang collection. They had to shoot them from a variety of angles: getting in and out of cars, walking through the plaza and of course the establishing shot in front of the fountain. The shoot itself was easy. The hard part was keeping would-be passersby from straying into the shots. After five long hours, they called it a wrap for the day.

"I figured as long as you didn't want to go out and celebrate we could celebrate, at home," Nick said to Danielle as they packed up their equipment. "Nice home-cooked meal, some champagne, and then I'll make love to you like I've been hungry to do all day." He winked at her.

"Sounds perfect." She screwed her lens cap on her camera and put it in its case, then hoisted it up on her shoulder by the strap.

"You could sound a little more enthusiastic."

"Sorry. Just a little headache."

"Hmm, we have some Tylenol at home, but if you can't wait, we can stop and get something."

She waved off his offer. "No. I'll be okay. Just the sun, the work and all the excitement. I'll be fine."

Nick stared at her a moment, then took her by the shoulders and turned her to face him. "You want to tell me what's going on with you?"

"I don't know what you mean."

"I mean, the way you're acting. Like… I don't know, like you're hiding something."

She made a face. "Hiding something," she echoed. "Don't be silly."

"Hey, whatever. When the real Danielle Holloway gets back, let me know. I'm going to the gym." He walked off toward his car, got behind the wheel and drove off.

Danielle's shoulders slumped as if the air had been let out of her. She couldn't go on lying to Nick, but what choice did she have? Maybe this whole TLC thing wasn't for her after all. Yet it was something she felt compelled to do from deep down inside. It wasn't the case itself. It was about proving to herself that she could be so much more than just a pretty face, someone's girlfriend, good in bed. It would provide personal satisfaction to take on something challenging, something that didn't come easily to her, like everything else in her life. She'd always gotten a pass because of how she looked. Most times it had nothing to do with her ability. And a part of her always felt inadequate as a result. This was different. She knew that it would challenge her relation-

ship with Nick. But it was a risk she needed to take—
for herself.

She waved goodbye to her crew and the models and
headed to her ride. Then it hit her. Nick was going to
the gym. She knew his routine. He would go home,
drop off his equipment, change into his exercise gear,
then head out. He'd be gone at least three hours. She
checked her watch. It was six forty-five. If she played
it right, she could be home from her meeting before
Nick got back from the gym.

She hopped behind the wheel of her vehicle, pulled
out her BlackBerry and dialed Savannah.

"I have a real short window," she said, checking
before pulling out into traffic. "Nick is going to the gym."

"Great."

"How long do you think this will take?"

"No more than an hour. It's basically orientation,
signing confidentiality papers, getting contact info and
the CD with TLC information on it."

Danielle blew out a breath. "Okay. I can manage that."

"Call me later and let me know how it went."

"I will."

Danielle disconnected the call and headed across
town. Hopefully, Nick had gone to his own gym down
in the West Village and not Pause for Men.

The last of the rush-hour traffic extended Danielle's
half-hour drive to nearly an hour. It was all the residual
effects of the U.N. Summit, which had tied the city in
knots for almost a week.

She eased onto 135th Street in Harlem, on the
lookout for any signs of Nick's car. She pulled the Navi-

gator around the corner and parked. It was only seven forty. She hoped Ms. Jean "Rules and Regulations" Wallington-Armstrong didn't mind her being early.

She approached the corner and stopped dead in her tracks. Bernard Hassell was crossing the street in the direction of Pause for Men. His back was almost to her, but if he turned his head, she'd be right in his line of vision. She took several steps backward, ducked around the corner and watched him from the side of the building until he'd gone inside.

Her heart was pounding so hard in her chest that she could barely breathe. For a moment she shut her eyes and shook her head. This was crazy, she thought, before easing around the corner. She hurried to the building, intermittently checking the house across the street. At the downstairs door she rang the bell, and the few seconds that ticked by seemed like an eternity.

"Good evening, Ms. Holloway. Nice to see you again," Margaret said. "Jean is waiting for you. Go right up. Do you remember the way?" she asked, stepping aside to let Danielle in.

"Yes, I'm pretty sure I remember. Are you here…full-time?" Danielle asked as they entered the foyer.

"You could say that. With all that's going on in the world, solving its problems is a full-time job." She stopped at the bottom of the staircase. Danielle turned to her. "Good luck," Margaret said with a wise smile. "You'll be fine." She turned and walked away.

I sure as hell hope so, Danielle thought as she walked upstairs.

When Danielle approached the door, she could hear

Jean talking to someone. She didn't hear anyone else and realized she was on the phone. For an instant she debated about announcing herself or listening for a minute. Her curiosity won out.

"...I understand that. Is there really a reason to get Homeland Security involved? I see. You know I'll help in any way that I can on the local level. You do understand that the people I'm working for on this case cannot be involved. It's the reason why I was hired. Of course. Keep me posted and I'll do the same."

What the hell was that about? Danielle wondered. She stepped up to the door and knocked.

"Come in."

She entered as Jean was hanging up the phone.

"Close the door, please."

Danielle did as she was asked, crossed the room and sat down.

"This shouldn't take long," Jean said, a line of worry bunching her brows together. She went to a file cabinet on the far side of the room and took out a thick folder, then brought it to her desk. She flipped the folder open and put on her pink-framed glasses.

"We've completed our background check on you Danielle, and for the most part everything came back fine." She extracted several photographs and pushed them across the table.

It was a series of pictures of her with Savannah and Mia at The Shop, her and Nick several weeks ago on one of their evening walks, her getting into her SUV, and even a photograph from that morning of her visit to Michael Preston's studio.

Her eyes flashed at Jean. "You've been following me?"

"Of course." She pushed another document across the table. It was her credit report and another series of papers detailing her entire life, everything from where she lived to the schools she'd attended, her parents' information and the loan from the bank to get her business operational.

"It's very easy to find out anything you want about someone. It's the business we're in. And of course we had to be sure that your lifestyle and your associations wouldn't hamper your ability to do this job. I'm sure you understand."

Danielle didn't know what she understood or what she thought. She felt so violated that she was speechless.

"Any questions?"

Danielle blinked. "No," she murmured.

"Good." She opened her desk drawer and took out a very legal-looking document and passed it to Danielle. "Please look this over, and if you agree, I'll need your signature."

It was pretty much what Savannah described: a confidentiality statement in addition to a clause that stated if she were caught, the Cartel would do what they could from behind the scenes, but they would never acknowledge her association with them. Her temples began to pound.

If she was caught. Ugly images filled her head, first of old, dank warehouses with her inside—tied to a chair and being interrogated by men in dark clothes and indistinguishable features—filled her head, then of a two-bunk cell that she shared with a woman whose nickname was Big Bertha and, finally, being thrown from a speeding car onto some desolate road, where she'd be left for the vultures—man or beast.

She stared at the words until they blurred. Her and her big mouth. She could have said she was busy, too. She wouldn't have been lying. But, noooo, she had to volunteer and even asked for a gun. God, Savannah was her dearest friend, and she would do anything in the world for her, but this… Identity theft sounded mundane on the surface, but what if it wasn't?

What had she gotten herself into?

"Is there a problem?"

Jean's strident voice snapped the final thread that connected Danielle the woman she was to Danielle the woman she was crossing the threshold to becoming. If she signed her name, there was no turning back. For a moment she hung suspended, unsure whether to leap across or crawl back to the other side.

Danielle glanced at Jean, who was rolling a silver pen between her thin fingers—or was it a stake?—and she could swear she saw the word *coward* reflected in Jean's emerald-green eyes. But it was her own face.

Jean abruptly stood. "We can't use anyone in the Cartel who is unsure of themselves, Ms. Holloway. Too much is at stake, and it's apparent that this is not for you."

…that's one of the things I love about you, your fierce determination. Nick's words ejected her out of the abyss of doubt to which she'd momentarily sunk. This was about proving something to herself, to remove all the inward doubts that she harbored about her own validity.

She reached for the pen on the desk and signed with a flourish, then pushed the papers back across the desk.

She pinned Jean with a withering stare of her own. "That's where you're wrong."

Was that an inkling of a smile taunting Jean's barely there lips?

Jean put the form back in the folder, then looked at Danielle. "I'm assigning you to Margaret, who will give you a full history on the organization. She will set your schedule and monitor your progress. You're going to have to be trained in how to use all of the surveillance equipment. Once Margaret is satisfied, the details of your assignment will be given to you. I cannot impress upon you enough that under no circumstance are you to ever divulge anything about TLC to anyone—that includes Nick Mateo." She paused. "Are we clear?"

"Yes."

"Good." She stood. "Margaret will give you the information that you need on your way out."

Danielle got up. "Thank you." She turned to leave.

Jean watched her as she walked out and hoped that she hadn't made a mistake. The truth was, their resources were stretched thin. If she'd had her way, she would have gotten someone else. But she'd made promises and she had to fulfill them.

Margaret was waiting for Danielle in the main room on the parlor floor.

"That wasn't so bad, now, was it?" she asked with that secret gleam in her eyes.

Danielle drew in a breath. "I guess that depends on what you call bad." She forced a nervous smile.

"Come with me. I have some things to go over with you."

* * *

A little more than an hour later, Danielle was walking out of the door of the Cartel headquarters and surreptitiously heading toward her car, keeping a corner of an eye out for any signs of Bernard Hassell.

Once behind the wheel she breathed a sigh of relief. The time on the dash read eight forty-five. If she hurried, she knew she would beat Nick home; maybe she would order something fancy from a local restaurant for dinner and use her feminine wiles to make up to him for being so unreceptive earlier.

She turned the key in the ignition in concert with a sharp knock on her window that jerked her an inch off her seat.

Oh, damn! She turned down the window. "Nick."

Chapter 6

Savannah pushed open the door to her town house and couldn't wait to get out of her shoes. Even though she was only in her first trimester and tried to remember to put her feet up whenever she could during the day, they were still swollen. Not badly, but enough to be just a little uncomfortable. Her one nightmare about this pregnancy was that with her being a petite five foot three that she would blow up to whale size and have to wear ugly balloon clothes and special shoes, instead of the jazzy designer maternity outfits she'd spent a zillion dollars on. She carried her shoes in one hand and her purse in the other, padding barefoot to her bedroom.

She took off her suit jacket and tossed it on the bed. Her shirt, bra and panties shortly followed.

"Whew, that feels good."

Savannah plopped down on the side of the bed and massaged her feet and wished that Danielle was around. A week earlier she'd given her the best foot massage.

She sighed and wondered how Danielle was making out with her assignment. She felt responsible for however it turned out, since she had recommended Dani to Jean in the first place.

Had Savannah not been in her current condition, the case would have been hers, and she felt a little left out of the action. She loved the fact that she was finally pregnant after trying for so long, but her friends, her mother and even her workaholic boss, Richard, treated her like spun glass.

She squeezed her toes between her fingers. Sometimes what she wanted to do was jump out and tell them that less than a month earlier she'd been a superspy, taking down a major foundation!

She yawned loudly and rubbed her tummy. She really did want to help Dani the way she'd helped her. But the truth was all she could concentrate on for the most part was sleep, sex and sustenance—and not necessarily in that order, she thought with a smile.

Slowly she pushed herself up and caught a glimpse of her slightly rounding form in the mirror that hung on the closet door. She turned from side to side, admiring the added plumpness of her behind and the fullness of her breasts.

The bedroom door pushed open. Savannah turned.

Blake's dark eyes darkened even more. His so very kissable mouth moved into a slow smile. He closed the door and moved toward his wife.

"Damn, baby," he said in a low growl. "You could make a man crazy coming home to look at you like this."

Savannah's body heated. Her heart pounded. "Like what?" she said, her voice laced with a desire for the man in front of her that never seemed to leave.

Blake moved closer, tugging at his tie. "Lush, sexy as all hell, beautiful." He was right on her now, the cotton fabric of his shirt brushing against her very tender nipples, sending jolts of electricity rushing through her. His fingertips trailed across her baby bump. "And filled with our child." He lowered his head and kissed her so tenderly, Savannah felt like weeping. "I love you so much," he uttered against her mouth.

Savannah was on fire and knew that if her husband didn't make love to her right then and there, she was going to implode. Her fingers fumbled with the buttons of his shirt. He tugged it off while she unfastened his thin leather belt and unzipped him.

They moved in unison to their bed, with Savannah landing on top of him. He cupped her breasts, their fullness overflowing in his hands. Savannah moaned, spread her thighs on either side of him, bent her knees and positioned herself over his erection, which was throbbing against her.

She slid down on him, her wet heat enveloping him like a glove.

"Ohhhh," Blake cried out. His eyes squeezed shut. He grabbed her behind and pushed upward.

Savannah tossed her head back as a strangled cry gurgled up from her throat. The indescribable sensations that pulsed through every fiber of her being each time

Blake moved inside her made her head spin. She felt outside herself, as if she were floating on a bed of pleasure and her body was a receptacle for delight.

She rotated her hips, then thrust her pelvis forward. The tendons in Blake's neck stretched tautly. He looked into her eyes, his breath rushing through his partially opened mouth. He rose up, took the tip of her left nipple between his lips and teased it with the tip of tongue then grazed it with her teeth. Savannah began to tremble, from the balls of her feet, up the backs of her thighs, to pulse in the rise and fall of her behind, grip her spine and shake it.

"Come on, baby," Blake urged in a voice coated in lust. "Bring it." He grabbed her tightly by the hips so that she was unable to move, only able to take what he gave her—slow, deep, rotating thrusts that had her whimpering and shuddering. Tears of sublime pleasure sprang from her eyes.

"That's how we like it, right, baby?" he moaned.

"Yessss," she said through her teeth. She snatched his hands away and pressed them against her breasts as she took them to unbelievable heights with quick swirls of her lower body to meet his every push and pull.

Their incomprehensible sounds of pleasure filled the room, taking them higher and higher until they both exploded like rockets on the Fourth of July.

Savannah collapsed on top of Blake, both of them breathing hard and ragged.

Blake cuddled with her close to him, gently stroking her back, whispering his love for her in her ear and she whispering it back.

Life didn't get better than this. If only every couple

could be as happy as she and Blake, Savannah thought as she felt herself drifting off into the sleep of the satiated—just as the phone rang.

Savannah buried her head deeper into Blake's chest, but it didn't stop the ringing. Blake stretched his long arm across the bed and snatched up the phone.

"Hello?" he said, sounding sleepy. "Hey, Mom. Yeah, uh, she's right here."

Savannah flipped onto her back, mouthed "sorry" to her husband and took the phone.

"Mom. Hi." She listened for a few minutes, her eyes widening, followed by a frown. "Are you kidding me?"

Blake propped himself up on his elbow and looked with concern at Savannah.

"I… I don't know what to say. I mean…if you're happy, that's what's important. Sure. Okay, I'll talk to you tomorrow." Dreamlike, she hung up the phone and turned to Blake. "Mom and Bernard are getting married, and she wants me to help plan the wedding."

"I was hoping to see you." Danielle said, thinking fast. Her heart was banging so hard in her chest that she knew Nick could hear it.

"Really? What made you come over here instead of to my regular spot at Gold's Gym?"

"You said how much you liked this place. I just took a wild guess."

He looked at her for a long moment, as if trying to see something behind her words. "Lucky guess." He grinned and the line of tension between them snapped. "Look, I'm sorry about earlier."

"Me, too." She unbuckled her seat belt and got out. She stood in front of him, reached up and stroked his face. "Are you going to be long?"

"About an hour." He paused. "But I can come home now if you want."

Danielle smiled. "I'd like that," she said softly.

He kissed her lips and ran his hand along her hair that hung down her back. "See you at home."

Danielle got back into her Navigator and watched as Nick walked off to his Trailblazer. She let out a long breath of relief, realizing she was shaking all over, and gripped the steering wheel and stared off into space. She was going to have to be supercareful if she was to get through this without getting caught.

Danielle and Nick arrived at the same time and parked behind each other on the narrow street. Nick set the alarm on his vehicle and met up with Danielle at the top of the stairs to their apartment.

"I was really surprised to see you," he said, unlocking the front door. "For a minute I thought you were following me or something…or meeting someone."

She almost choked on that one.

Nick stepped aside to let her in and followed her up the steps. She kept her gaze focused on her feet.

"I felt bad and silly for being such a witch this afternoon. Especially when you were only being sweet." She glanced over her shoulder. "Like you always are."

She opened the door to their second-floor apartment, tossed her bag on the table in the foyer and turned to Nick, stopping him in his tracks.

Her eyes moved across his face. "I'm glad I found you," she said softly.

Nick slid his arms around her waist. "Tonight or in general?" he teased.

"Both."

"I'm glad I found you, too, Dani." He drew in a breath. "You're everything I want in every way." He pushed a loose strand of hair away from her face. "You know that?"

She looked up into his eyes. "Yes, I do." She rested her head on his chest and listened for a moment to the comforting beat of his heart. Why couldn't she totally commit to this man? she asked herself for the countless time.

Nick leaned back. "We got some great shots today before you arrived."

"Let's take a look while we fix something to eat. I'm suddenly ravenous."

"You mean, while I fix something to eat, don't you?"

She made a face and poked him in the arm. "Whatever."

Nick chuckled. "Come on."

Huddled together on their king-size bed, with a steaming plate of homemade chicken fajitas next to them, they reviewed the day's shoot on Nick's twenty-one-inch Mac.

"These are fantastic," Danielle muttered over a mouthful of food. "Stephanie is incredible to work with. Wow, look at the way the light hits her accessories," she said, pointing to a shot of the model near the water fountain with the rush of Manhattan traffic in the background.

"And she knows exactly how to play up each piece without taking away from herself," Nick added.

"That's why she gets the megabucks," Danielle said drolly.

"Speaking of megabuck…" He hopped off the bed and left the room. Moments later he returned with two long-stemmed wineglasses and a bottle of champagne.

Danielle's eyes widened in delight. "What are you doing? And where did you find champagne?" she asked over her laughter.

He sauntered toward her and winked. "I always have a surprise up my sleeve. Well…actually," he hedged, "this was a gift from Mia when we went to her party a few months back."

"Ohhhh, right. I'd forgotten all about it."

"So had I." He sat on the side of the bed and after several attempts popped the cork with a flourish. The bubbling brew rushed to the top and spilled down the sides of the bottle neck.

They giggled as the champagne splashed over Nick's fingers and he stuck his head beneath the flow to catch it on his tongue.

Danielle held out her glass and he filled it. The bubbles tickled her nose, but the expensive champagne went down like silk.

"Mmmm, good stuff," she said.

Nick placed the bottle on the nightstand. He raised his glass. "To the new 'it' girl in the photography world." He touched his glass to hers.

"To *our* continued success," she said. "I couldn't have done it without you." She leaned forward and kissed him.

Nick took her glass from her hand and set it on the table next to the bed. He gazed into her eyes as he unbuttoned her blouse and slipped it from her shoulders. "Do you want this?" he asked, dropping featherlike kisses along the crests of her breasts.

Danielle's body shuddered. "Yes," she whispered.

He lowered one strap of her bra and then the other before pushing it down below the swell of her breasts so that they rose even higher.

"You're so beautiful," he said, his tone growing thick with desire.

"You make me feel beautiful all the time."

"I never want you to forget how much I adore you, Dani," he said in a ragged voice and eased her back against the thick pillows.

She draped her hands behind his head and urged him toward her mouth. His kiss was sweet, tender and possessive all at once, and Danielle lost herself in the bliss of it, giving him everything he gave her.

Their tongues danced the waltz, slow and sure; then they dueled in a tango and whined with the rhythm of the Caribbean.

She tugged at the hem of his gray T-shirt, and Nick needed no further coaxing. He pulled it over his head and tossed it on the floor.

Danielle's heart banged against her chest, and the bud between her thighs thickened and pulsed. Just looking at Nick's body was the ultimate turn-on. His devout exercise regime had rewarded him with the body of a god. His arms were like steel, and whenever he wrapped them around her, she knew she was safe and protected.

His chest was defined and rock hard, and it led down to a six-pack-like stomach that would make Mr. America weep in shame.

Through a series of maneuvers, they discarded the rest of their clothing and rolled around on the bed, laughing and finding places on each other's body to nibble, stroke and kiss until Danielle found herself pinned beneath Nick's weight.

"Don't move," he ordered, before inching his way down her body, starting at the pulse beat in her throat. He suckled her there until she began to squirm with pleasure. "Don't move," he said again. His tongue flicked across the tip of her hardened nipple, and a moan pushed through her lips. She grabbed a handful of sheet as he continued to lick and draw her nipple into his mouth, slowly and firmly.

Her stomach muscles fluttered and the inside of her thighs trembled. She gripped the sheets tighter as he neared her belly button and took a little dip.

Nick's strong fingers stroked her hips and thighs before pushing her legs apart.

"You sure you want this?" he asked, taunting her.

She couldn't speak. Her body was on fire. She nodded vigorously.

"I'll take that as a yes."

His thumb brushed across her wet, swollen pearl, and her hips instinctively rose in response.

"Naughty girl," he said, before grabbing her hips in a viselike grip and pinning her to the mattress.

His expert tongue and lush lips separated her wet folds and played her like a master violinist, each stroke, flick, lick more intense than the other. He drew the bud tenderly into his mouth and sucked on it until her cries filled the room in sweet agony.

Her head thrashed back and forth as bolts of electricity ran up and down her legs. She wanted to buck up against him, to push her essence even farther into his waiting mouth, but she couldn't move—and that reality only intensified her need and the experience.

Tears squeezed from the corners of her closed eyes when suddenly Nick released his grip on her and draped her legs over his neck, cupping her lush rear in his palms, and he went at her like a man hungry for dessert.

Danielle's thoughts spun while jolt after jolt of pleasure surged through her veins, and just as she was on the brink of release, Nick stopped. Her eyes shot open; her breath caught and held in her throat as she was suddenly filled with the hard thickness of him.

They both groaned in unison at the contact as Nick slid deep into her pulsing walls.

Nick held her like a bundled baby, crooning softly in her ear, professing his love and need for her as their bodies rose in ecstasy.

Danielle felt electrified as her limbs stiffened, her toes curled and her hips arched, thrusting hard and fast against each of Nick's downward strokes.

Then, like a volcanic eruption, she came, the sublime pleasure spewing from her lips in a rush of incoherent sounds of release that pushed Nick over the edge to fill her to her core with all the love he felt for her.

They lay together, still linked, their breathing exhaling in short erratic bursts while their heart rate slowed almost in unison.

"Congratulations," Nick murmured before sucking on her bottom lip, a glint of delight in his eyes.

Danielle giggled. "I think the congratulations should go to you, sir. That was quite a performance."

"Aw, shucks." He grinned. "Yeah, well, I *was* pretty good, if I have to say so myself."

She pinched his bare butt. He feigned a yelp and rolled off her and onto his back.

"You weren't half bad either," he said, still teasing her.

Danielle rolled her eyes, then snuggled against him. She draped her arm across his hard belly and nestled her head between his neck and shoulder.

"I was thinking that maybe we could take a weekend off and get away somewhere," Nick said.

Danielle tensed. "Hmm, sounds good."

"How 'bout next weekend?"

Her thoughts raced. "Well, let's see how things start off with this new account. There's no telling what is going to be required until we get that under wraps."

Nick blew out a breath, and Danielle fully expected him to reject the delay.

"You're probably right," he conceded. "Plus we still have the catalog work for JCPenney and the new shots for Ford Models."

She shut her eyes with relief. "True. So as soon as we can see some daylight, okay?"

"Sure." He rolled onto his side to face her. "As long as I get to spend some alone time with you." He kissed her shoulder. "I'm going to get some of the prints ready." He got off the bed.

"Okay," she said with a drawn-out sigh. "I'll just lie right here."

Nick laughed. "You do that." He wagged his finger. "Then you'll be well rested when I get back."

Once she was alone, she closed her eyes and all of her near misses for the day flashed behind her lids. She knew that Nick would be a while in their workroom, so she took the opportunity to check out the TLC video on her laptop.

The thirty-minute infomercial narrated by Jean Armstrong told of the beginnings of TLC and the reason why an organization that could function under the radar was necessary. They could go places that the police and government officials couldn't. She told of building the Cartel from former CIA and Homeland Security agents. All women, all highly skilled, all above suspicion. But Jean had envisioned an even more covert way to infiltrate the unsuspecting: train ordinary women who had innate, savvy and useful skills.

There were several links detailing many of the assignments that had been fulfilled since the organization's inception five years earlier, as well as short demonstrations of the tools of the trade: recording and listening devices, fingerprint tools, telephoto lens cameras and guns. All of which came in every TLC member's handy little makeup case.

Overall, it gave Danielle a sense of belonging to something greater than herself, and she felt the loyalty among the women whose stories were detailed on the presentation.

Throughout her childhood she'd never felt that she

belonged anywhere. She'd spent much of her life trying to fit in. Her mixed heritage had been a burden that constantly reared its ugly head in a world that held appearance in the highest esteem.

She remembered going to family gatherings on her mother's side of the family, which was Hispanic. Her father never went, and it wasn't until one afternoon that she found out why. She was sitting in the kitchen with her grandmother helping to prepare the standard rice and beans for dinner. Danielle adored her grandmother, and loved the times she spent with her, hanging on her every word. If her grandma said so, then it was so, as far as Danielle was concerned.

"You are such a beautiful girl," her grandmother had said as she poured a cup of coconut juice into the pot. "You take after your mother." She placed the cover on the pot and turned to her granddaughter. "Thank God for that." She shook her head.

"What do you mean, Ma Ma?"

Her grandmother turned to her, her sharp features pulled taut by the salt-and-pepper bun that she religiously wore like a badge of honor.

She wagged a finger at Danielle. "I told your mother not to marry that man. He wasn't good enough for her. But she wouldn't listen."

"I don't understand."

"Mixing," she said as if that would explain everything.

Danielle looked at her, curiously waiting for an explanation.

"Your father, he is not one of us. Black." She spat the

word out as if it would poison her if she didn't get rid of it quickly.

Danielle was blindsided by confusion.

"You could have turned out looking just like him. Black. With a big nose, thick lips and knotty hair." She breathed in relief. "But thank God—" she made a sign of the cross "—you didn't. I can't imagine what your life would have been like if you had." She went to the counter and began cutting up tomatoes for her special salsa. "Remember this if you remember nothing else, never marry anyone darker than a paper bag. If you do, I warn you, he will not be welcome in this family," she said with a haughty lift of her pointed chin.

The startling declaration from her grandmother had rocked Danielle to her core. She knew that she was different, that her mother and father were different from each other. It had never occurred to her that those differences had affected how the family viewed them, her grandmother in particular.

But those words stuck with Danielle and she began to see things that she hadn't seen before, or at least hadn't paid attention to. There was a time when she was out with her father in the supermarket. Her father had taken her hand and a woman strode right up to him and asked what he was doing with that little girl. He explained that she was his daughter. The woman looked from one to the other in blatant disbelief.

When she was out with her father they always got strange looks, but until that conversation with her grandmother, Danielle had never really noticed.

Then there were those rare occasions when they went

to Atlanta to visit her father's family. Her cousins would always tease her, pull her long hair and insist that she thought she was better than them. Invariably she wound up playing by herself. When her mother would ask her about it, she'd simply say that was what she wanted to do.

When her father would ask her to accompany him somewhere she began making excuses not to go.

As she moved into her teens and her natural beauty intensified, the distance between her and her father widened. She would look at him and feel ashamed.

Memories from her childhood haunted her, and there were many nights she lay awake next to Nick and wondered if what she felt for him was real or just easy.

Danielle heard Nick move from the workroom to the kitchen just as the CD was coming to an end.

She popped out the CD and closed the cover of her laptop just as Nick walked back into the room. The success of TLC hinged on its secrecy. It was a rule that was not to be broken.

"I thought you were resting." He tugged his T-shirt over his head and walked toward her.

"I was just making some notes for tomorrow." She forced a smile and palmed the CD, pushing the thoughts of her past into the background.

"What's that?"

"What?"

He jutted his chin in the direction of the CD. "That. In your hand."

"Oh, just a CD." She shrugged, hopped off the bed and dropped it in her purse.

She turned toward him. "Finished with the photos?"

"Yeah," he said absentmindedly. He slowly shook his head, then looked directly at her. "Are you seeing someone else?"

Chapter 7

"He actually asked you if you were seeing someone?" Savannah asked in disbelief. She lifted the cup of iced herb tea to her lips and took a sip.

"Yes. Would I make up something like that?" She took a long swallow of her mango and pineapple smoothie.

She'd called Savannah first thing in the morning after Nick had gone off to set up the shoot and had asked to meet at The Shop.

"What did you tell him?" She buttered her wheat toast.

"The truth! He kept insisting that I've been acting strange lately, and he's getting the feeling that he doesn't know who I am anymore. If it's like this now, what's going to happen once I get involved in the assignment— whatever the hell it is."

"Take it easy. Everything is going to be fine."

"I don't want to ruin my relationship over this. I haven't even started yet and it's already putting a strain on us."

"You won't have to. Nick is a great guy. He's not going to leave you." She paused for a moment. "Do you want to back out…because if you do, I'm sure Jean can find someone else."

"No." She reminded herself of all the reasons why she needed to do this. "When have you ever known me to back out of anything?"

"Are you sure?"

She hesitated for a moment. "Yes," she said on a long breath.

Savannah reached across the table and covered Danielle's hand. She looked into her friend's troubled eyes. "The only thing I can suggest, girlfriend, is to make it up to that man every chance you get."

Danielle half smiled at the innuendo.

"I have some stunning news myself."

"What?"

"My mother is getting married."

Danielle's dark brows shot upward. "Get. Outta. Here," she said, defining each word. "To Bernard?"

Savannah nodded slowly and took a bite of her toast. "I was so stunned I'm not sure I even congratulated her. She's only known him a couple of months. It's crazy."

"Wow" was all Danielle could manage. She had yet to tell Savannah about Bernard and Nick attending the spa right across the street from the Cartel. That was a sticky little problem she would work out on her own.

"Hey, your mom has plenty of sense. I'm sure she's in love with him," she offered.

"I guess," Savannah said, sounding unconvinced. "If the tables were turned, she'd have me on *Oprah* for some kind of counseling."

They laughed. Yes, that was something Claudia Martin would certainly do. When it came to her daughter, she was the definition of a lioness protecting her cub.

"Be happy for her, sweetie. Your dad has been dead a long time, and your mother has been alone."

"I know. I'm sure that's one of the reasons why she got involved with the Cartel in the first place—to fill those days and hours. It's just…I don't want her to be hurt. I mean, how much do we know about him anyway, other than the fact that he looks and sounds like Billy Dee Williams?"

Danielle twisted her lips. "That's true. But again, Claudia is a savvy woman. She'll be fine." She checked her watch. "Ouch, I gotta go before I have more explaining to do."

Savannah finished her tea. "Me, too."

They left the money on the table for their minibreakfast and stood.

"When do you start your training?" Savannah asked as they walked outside.

"I got the CD and went over it again this morning while Nick was in the shower. I start this evening."

"Great. You need a cover story for Nick?"

"We're not actually speaking at the moment. So I don't think I'll need one. He said he was going to stay at his apartment tonight."

Savannah could see the cloud of sadness around Danielle's eyes. "I didn't know he still had his place."

"Yeah. Even though he has most of his stuff at my place and we're together every night, he never gave up his spot in the Village." She laughed without humor. "Guess it was a good move on his part, huh?"

"It may seem awful at the moment, but let it work in your favor. Know what I mean."

"True. Well, let me get going." She kissed Savannah's cheek. "Oh, I forgot to tell you. I got the Michael Preston account. I'll be photographing his entire fall line."

Savannah's mouth opened to a perfect *O*. "Girl! Why didn't you tell me? Now that *is* major news." She grabbed Danielle in a quick hug. "Congratulations."

Danielle smiled a real smile for the first time that morning. "I'm excited."

"You should be. We must celebrate. As soon as Mia gets back."

"Definitely."

"Okay, gotta run. Love ya, girl, and don't worry."

Danielle finger-waved as Savannah got in her car. She turned in the opposite direction and walked the half block to reach hers.

She would find a way to make this all work, she decided as she got into her vehicle. She would do her job, manage the Preston account, do her Cartel thing, win back her man and fry up some bacon while she was at it.

Danielle smiled to herself as she put the SUV in gear. *After all, I am woman,* she thought, before dramatically slipping on her designer shades and pulling out into traffic. *Hear me roar.*

* * *

All things considered, the day on location went by relatively smoothly. Nick was polite and professional, if a little indifferent.

Danielle caught him looking at her several times when he thought she wasn't watching, and she caught the look of longing and maybe a bit of sadness around his indigo eyes.

As much as she wanted to go over to him, wrap him in her arms and tell him how sorry she was, she knew it would be a bad move on her part. They would make up, he'd come back to her place and it would ruin her night of training.

So, as much as it hurt her, she played the indifferent role as well.

"Good day today," Nick said as they packed up their gear.

"Yes, very." She kept her eyes focused on her camera as she placed it in the case.

"So, uh, I guess I'll see you tomorrow."

"Today's a wrap, remember?"

"Oh…right."

She watched his throat bob up and down as if the words were stuck there.

She hoisted her carryall on her right shoulder. "Guess I'll see you…next week."

"Yeah…I guess," he said, his voice barely above a whisper.

She turned to leave, her eyes burning and her heart pounding. A part of her wanted him to come after her, tell her he was coming home. The other part of her dreaded it, knowing what it would mean. She lifted her head a notch higher and walked to her vehicle.

Danielle arrived at the brownstone without incident and spent the next two hours with Margaret learning the intricacies of the surveillance equipment. Cameras were not an issue, so they were able to bypass that lesson.

Margaret had her set up the magnetic listening devices in several of the rooms. Then Margaret went to see how well they'd been placed and how good the transmission was.

"You catch on very quickly," Margaret said as she placed the dime-size receiver back in the box.

"Thanks."

"You may or may not need to use these, but it's always an excellent skill to have." Margaret opened another compartment in the makeup case and took out what looked like a manicure set. In actuality, it was burglary tools.

For the next half hour, Margaret showed her how to open different types of locks without detection on a set of doors that were installed for that purpose down in the basement of the brownstone.

"It's all about touch," Margaret said as Danielle worked the razor-thin tools in the lock. "Concentrate and remember to press your fingertips around the lock. You can feel the tumblers move. Very similar to breaking into a safe," she said matter-of-factly.

Danielle stole a glance over her shoulder and looked at Margaret's serene expression, waiting for her to say she was only kidding. But she could tell by the even set of her lips that she wasn't. She turned back to the task at hand, and several moments later the door clicked open.

Danielle stood, turned to Margaret and beamed in delight.

"Excellent. A few more tries and you can get it under a minute. That's the goal," she added with a wag of her finger. "One last thing before we end the lesson for today." She led Danielle back upstairs to the computer center on the top floor of the four-story building.

Danielle was blown away when Margaret opened the door to a room filled with the latest in computer technology. There was a digital map of the world on the wall with pulsating green lights highlighting different locations. Several women wearing headsets with microphones attached sat in front of large computer screens. The hum of electronics buzzed in the air. It looked like a room right out of a *Mission: Impossible* movie.

"This is the nerve center of the Cartel," Margaret explained as she gave her a short tour. "We can track any of our members, contact them at any time and keep a pinpoint on all of the ongoing cases anywhere around the world right from this room. In addition, any tracking device put on a vehicle or an individual is monitored from this room. It's soundproof and all of the computers are programmed to self-destruct the information contained on the hard drives should that become necessary."

Danielle was impressed.

"Our spyware is developed here as well." She pointed to a woman who looked to be no more than twenty-five.

"Jasmine is one of the techies who designed the 'hello dolly' virus that shut down Regency Airlines three years ago. Disastrous for the airline, but it was quite brilliant. She spent about a year in jail, but the government felt she would be much more effective working for us than for them." She walked over to Jasmine and introduced her to Danielle.

"She is our newest recruit but is on a fast-track training regime. I need you to show her how to install one of the keystroke viruses on the computer and how to connect her audio and video recorders to come up on her PDA and her personal computer."

"Sure thing. Have a seat."

"I'll see you in about an hour," Margaret said and left.

Jasmine was not only brilliant but also funny, and she had Danielle cracking up about some of the antics she'd pulled on the computer.

"Where did you learn all this stuff?" Danielle asked as she plugged in her PDA to the computer with a USB cable.

"I think I was born with a love for gadgets," she said, pushing her thin, wire-framed glasses farther up the bridge of her narrow nose. "I've been taking things apart for as long as I can remember. Electronics fascinate me."

Danielle looked at the screen on her PDA and was thrilled to find a live video of the inside of the very room they were in.

Jasmine grinned. "I think you've got it."

Danielle bobbed her head in delighted agreement.

* * *

On the drive home she went over all the things she'd learned in one evening. She was sure there was much more to it, but at least she had the basics. She'd do more reading at home and watch the second CD that she'd gotten from Margaret on her way out.

At least she could stay busy and keep her mind occupied and off Nick.

The mere mention of his name in her thoughts made the muscles in her stomach clench. She missed him already, and it could only get worse before it got better.

When she walked into her apartment, the familiar sound of Nick's off-key singing and the scent of something scrumptious in the air were missing.

A wave of sadness washed over her. Since she'd allowed herself to believe that she actually deserved a happy relationship, she'd let Nick into her heart, her spirit. That was something she'd avoided for much too long of a time, and for reasons that she didn't want to even think about.

She had relationship issues, she knew that. How could she truly love anyone else when she didn't love herself? Sure, she went through the motions with the men she'd met. Most, if not all, were always attracted to how she looked. She'd become so jaded by it that she treated men the same way. Good looks and great sex—that was all she needed or wanted. But Nick's love and patience were slowly beginning to climb over the walls she'd erected around her emotions. And that scared her. It had been so long since the wall went up that she had no idea what was on the other side anymore, or if there was anything worth finding. And that was why this assignment was so important to her, even at the risk of damaging her relationship with Nick. She had something to prove to herself, that she was so much more than an image. And Nick's words of adoration and support were not enough. She must discover it for herself if she was to ever be the woman that he deserved.

Slowly she walked through the empty apartment. She could almost feel his presence, smell his scent. She went into the bedroom, tossed her things on the bed and followed right behind them.

What if he didn't come back? she thought, the rush of misery running over her like an unwanted icy shower. There had to be a quick way out of this mess she'd gotten herself into. The truth of the matter was, she wanted her cake and she wanted to eat it, too.

The phone rang, jerking her up from the bed. She scrambled across the mattress. If it was Nick, she was going to tell him to come home—no matter what. Maybe she'd even say the *L* word if that was what it took.

She snatched up the receiver and calmed herself because she didn't want to sound too eager. "Hello?" Her heart pounded.

"Danielle, please."

Her spirits shrank to a level right below the bottom of the soles of her shoes.

"Speaking."

"This is Jean Armstrong."

Danielle sat up straight on the bed. "Yes, Ms. Armstrong." She cleared her throat.

"I just concluded my meeting with Margaret and Jasmine. I understand that you did extremely well."

"Thank you."

"Better than any new recruit we've seen in quite some time."

Her brows rose. "Really?"

"As a result I'd like you to stop by tomorrow and pick up your kit. You will be given the instructions about your assignment at that time. Come whenever it's convenient for you."

"Are you saying that I don't have to do any more training?"

"At some point you will, but for the purposes of this assignment you have a very good handle on what you will need to get it done. You see, dear, what we rely on more than technology from our Cartel members are determination and ingenuity. You have both."

"Thank you. That means a great deal."

"Tomorrow, then. Welcome to the Cartel."

"Thanks."

"Oh, and by the way, Danielle, it was a brave thing you did to allow Nick to go back to his apartment. Not many women would be willing to risk that. Actually, it was the deciding factor in allowing you to join us."

"W-what," she sputtered. "How could you know that?"

"Believe me, my dear, I know everything. And always remember that Cartel members don't have a label on their foreheads. They look just like me and you.

That's the whole point, isn't it? Rest well. And not to worry, he'll be back."

The next thing Danielle knew the dial tone was humming in her ear. Dreamlike, she hung up the phone.

How could she know those things? Was one of her photography team members part of the Cartel? One of the models? Did Savannah say something to Jean?

She didn't know whether to be furious or scared out of her thong. It was beyond creepy that someone could know those kinds of intimate details about a person without their knowledge. But like Jean said, that was the whole point.

Slowly the threads of excitement began to wind their way through her veins. However complex the assignment, she would handle it, and since Jean seemed to know everything, Nick would be back as well.

She only hoped, on that note, that it wouldn't be the one time Jean was wrong.

Chapter 8

Nick was seated at the juice bar at the Pause for Men day spa when Bernard slid onto the stool beside him. He clapped him on the back.

"Had a good workout?"

Nick angled his head to the left. "Yeah, pretty good."

Bernard signaled to the waitress, who came and took his order for a veggie burger and a shake. "So how are you liking this place so far?"

"I like it a lot. You couldn't ask for more. The workout rooms are top-notch, customer service is great and you can't beat the food for the price."

Bernard chuckled. "So do you think you want to join, or are you going to live out your guest privileges?"

Nick lowered his head and grinned. "Yeah, I plan to sign up. Actually I was going to do that today. The way things are going in my life I'm going to need all the de-stressing I can get—or afford."

"Something wrong? Maybe I can help. You look like you could use a friend or an ear. I'm pretty good at both." He gave the young man an encouraging smile.

Nick drew in a breath. When was the last time he'd expressed his feelings or his insecurities to anyone until he'd met Danielle? It had been so long since he'd had a man-to-man talk that he wasn't sure he knew how. But there was something about Bernard that made him feel safe and comfortable, as if they'd known each other for years.

He angled his body toward Bernard. His words came out halting, as if he were testing out the language for the first time.

"I guess I've always been pretty much a loner. I can't admit to having a best male buddy, just acquaintances, guys I hang out with from time to time." He swallowed, pausing for a moment in thought. "My best friend was my dad. When he died, I was only fourteen."

"I'm sorry," Bernard murmured.

Nick continued as if he didn't hear him. "We were together…when it happened." He stared off into space. His heart started racing like it always did when he thought about that day. "He took me to a baseball game at Shea Stadium. When we got back home, we were tossing the ball back and forth to each other. I missed one of his throws and—" his voice thickened "—it went into the street. Stupid me, I went running after it. I never even heard him yell for me to look out. The next thing I knew, I was thrown onto the sidewalk and my dad was in the middle of the street nearly half a block away. The car that missed me hit him." He took a swallow of his smoothie to keep Bernard from seeing the tears that were burning his eyes. "I don't think my mother ever forgave me. She never came right out and said that it was my fault, but I could see it in her eyes every time she looked at me. I moved out the day after high-school graduation.

"I've never allowed myself those kinds of attachments again. And I know that a lot of how I feel about myself stems from back then. After he died, I didn't know where I fit. I look like my dad, with his strong Italian features, dark hair and eyes and swarthy complexion. So I identified with him, even though my mother's African-American blood runs through my veins, too." He turned his head toward Bernard. "I was lost, just going through the motions until I met Danielle. And now I think she's seeing someone else." He finished off his drink.

"Why would you think that?"

"All the signs are there."

"It could be a lot of things. That's pretty extreme, don't you think? I mean, I've only met her a couple of times, but when I see her look at you, I can't imagine that she looks at anyone else like that."

Nick sputtered a derisive chuckle. "Thanks for the ego boost."

"I wasn't trying to boost your ego, son, I'm just telling you what I see. Take it from one who knows, the woman is in love with you."

"That's where you're wrong. She can barely get the words to frame in her head, least of all say them," he said, the hurt and disappointment tainting his voice.

"It's not about the words. It's about what's in here." He tapped his chest.

Nick laced his fingers together on top of the counter and studied his knuckles. "I never told Dani any of that stuff," he said, so quietly Bernard almost missed it.

"Why don't you talk to her about how you feel? The same way you told me. I think you would be surprised."

"Maybe." He drew himself up, forcing a bright expression on his face. "If you want to get me to sign up with this joint, you'd better catch me now," he said, pushing the conversation and the past into the back of his mind.

Just then the waitress returned with his food.

"I'm sorry. Can you hang on to that for me for a bit—keep it warm? I'll be right back."

"Sure, Bernie."

"Thanks, doll."

"No problem."

Bernard cocked his head toward the registration counter. "Come on, I'll introduce you to the owners. There are only three of them now. One of the original owners, Barbara Allen, moved down south with her new husband."

They stepped up to the horseshoe-shaped desk. "Evenin', ladies," Bernard said to the trio, who had gathered at the counter which was their routine at the end of each evening.

The three were as different as apples, oranges and grapes, Nick observed. One was a stunning petite beauty, barely reaching the shoulders of the other two; one could give Tyra Banks a run for her money; the third reminded him of Angela Bassett, with her wide, open smile and dancing eyes.

"Hey, Bernie," Ann Marie greeted him, followed by Elizabeth and Stephanie.

"I wanted you ladies to meet a new recruit, Nick Mateo."

The Tyra Banks runner-up stuck out her hand. "Stephanie Moore. I'm *supposed* to be the publicist promoting the spa, but it looks like Bernie is after my job." She laughed good-naturedly and winked at Bernard.

Then it was the tiny dynamo. "Ann Marie Dennis, Girl Friday, and the one responsible for securing this building. In my other life I do real estate, so if you're ever in the market, be sure to let me know," she said, with what Nick noticed as a slight Caribbean accent.

"Elizabeth Lewis. I'm the general manager. I actually live on the top floor."

"Yes, she luck out and catch de man who fixin' up de whole damn place," Ann Marie said, laying on her accent hot and heavy. She pursed her lips in feigned annoyance. "Me have to go all the way home to me man. All she 'ave to do is run upstairs. Ya call dat fair?"

The trio chuckled.

Nick couldn't help but laugh.

"Don't hate, as the kids would say," Elizabeth said calmly.

"Anyway," Stephanie cut in. "Don't mind them. It's an everyday thing with those two. So how can I help you?"

"I *think* I want to sign up for membership," Nick said over the remnants of his laughter.

"The more the merrier," Ann Marie said. "Well, folks, I'm heading home to Sterling. See you tomorrow." She turned to Nick. "Nice to meet you. I'm sure you'll enjoy being here. And any friend of Bernard's is a friend of ours." She wagged her fingers and sauntered off, and it was then that Nick noticed that she had on at least three-inch heels and was still no bigger than a minute.

"I'll leave you to take care of your business. I'll be in the café when you're done," Bernie said.

"Sure." He took a seat in one of the leather pedestal chairs, while Stephanie took out some of the brochures and Elizabeth pulled out the paperwork.

"Wanna grab a beer?" Bernard asked as he and Nick left Pause for Men.

Did he really want to go home to a tiny, empty apartment and lie awake, staring at the ceiling, for the rest of the night?

"Sure. Why not?"

"Great. If you don't mind walking a few blocks, we can go to the Lenox Lounge."

"Sounds great. I haven't been there since—" His thought skidded to a stop. The last time he was there was with Danielle. "—in a while," he finished.

As they strolled through Harlem, the sights and sounds of the famous district surrounded them. Even though many of the historical spots such as Small's Paradise, Copelands, Sugar Hill and other after-hours locales and restaurants were long gone, there was still a pulse, a vitality that one could feel in the air.

They pushed through the doors of the Lenox Lounge

and were surprised to find the place packed on a week-night. Inching their way to the end of the bar, they squeezed in.

The barmaid came down to meet them. "What'll you have?"

"Two beers. Whatever you have on tap," Bernard shouted over the noise of voices and music. The aroma of fried chicken wafted in the air. "What's going on tonight? It's pretty crowded."

"New singer, Dawne. Young sister from Brooklyn. Sounds like a young Aretha. We've been promoting her all week." She expertly filled two mugs to the brim and placed them on the counter. "Four bucks each."

Nick went into his pocket.

Bernard stopped him with a hand on his wrist. "I got it."

"Thanks."

They took their beers to the back room, just as the first set was getting started. As promised, the little powerhouse was a young Aretha in the making who earned the respect and rousing applause of the audience.

By the time they left nearly two hours later, Nick was in a much better frame of mind. They strolled back to their cars, talking about a little bit of everything along the way.

Bernard told Nick about his growing-up years in St. Albans, in Queens, New York, and Nick shared more of his life in Staten Island before moving to Manhattan.

"Hey, I hope you'll come to my wedding," Bernard said.

"Wedding?" Nick asked, stopping in front of his car.

Bernard grinned. "Yeah, I popped the question to Claudia, and she said yes."

Nick stuck out his hand, which Bernard heartily shook. He was beaming like a kid on Christmas.

"Congratulations. I had no idea."

"It's all kind of new. She told Savannah last night."

Nick grinned. "Claudia is a great lady. You're a lucky man."

"When you find someone you love, you can't let them get away. You may not be as lucky the next time." He clapped Nick on the shoulder. "See you at the gym. Thanks for hanging out with an old man." He walked away.

Nick got in his vehicle and sat there for a few minutes, going over his evening with Bernard. He glanced at the time on the digital dash. It was nearly eleven thirty. He put the car in gear and slowly headed home.

Nick took his key out of his pocket and stuck it in the lock. As he'd expected, the apartment was quiet. He tucked his backpack in the hall closet and headed toward the bedroom.

He gently sat down on the side of the bed and leaned over and brushed a lock of hair away from Danielle's face. She stirred. Her eyes fluttered open, and she jerked partially upward and gasped in alarm.

"Shhh. It's me, baby." He leaned down and kissed the top of her head, and she all but crawled into his arms.

He squeezed her to him, stroking her back, and she held on as if she feared he would vanish like a dream upon awakening.

"I'm sorry," they said in unison, then laughed.

"I'm giving up my apartment tomorrow," he whispered in her ear. "I don't ever want there to be anywhere else I come home to but to you."

Danielle's heart swelled with emotion. Tears of relief and joy slipped from behind her closed lids.

"I don't want you to be anywhere else but here," she whispered.

"Are you sure?"

"I've never been more sure of anything in my life." She slid over in the bed and lifted the covers back.

Nick kicked off his shoes and spooned with her in the bed, not even bothering to get out of his clothes.

Danielle felt the warmth of his breath on her neck, the comfort of his arms around her, the security of the steady beat of his heart, and she knew that somehow things would be all right. She would do whatever she must to ensure it.

And then she felt Nick's hands begin to slowly explore her body, and the rush of anticipation began to fill her. Jean's closing words came to mind. *He'll be back.*

Jean was right, but it was now up to her to make certain that she didn't do anything to make him leave ever again.

She turned onto her back, cupped his face in her palms. "Let me show you how much I missed you," she said in a husky whisper.

"Whatever you say, baby."

She unzipped him and went to work.

Chapter 9

"Who was at the door?" Danielle asked the following morning as she stepped out of the bathroom.

"Oh, a messenger dropped off a box for you. I left it in the living room. Were you expecting a package?" Nick was busy staring at the computer screen and munching on a blueberry muffin.

"Hmm, no. Don't think so." She wrapped her wet hair in a towel and tightened the belt around her robe, then padded barefoot across the hardwood floors to the living room.

"Your breakfast is in the oven," he called out.

"Thanks!"

She saw the box right away, perched atop the hall table. Unable to imagine what it could be, she frowned, then checked for a name and didn't see one. She took the box over to the couch and began digging it open. Once the top was finally pulled off, her heart thumped. She stole a glance over her shoulder. Gingerly, she took the package out. It was the TLC Bath and Body carrying case.

She was so excited that she nearly squealed in anticipation. With a turn of the catch, the box opened. To the untrained eye the contents were no more sinister than eye shadows, makeup brushes, minidisks of lip gloss, body washes, oils and lotions. But she knew better. Each item had a dual purpose. She lifted the top layer of the case and nestled beneath was the outline of where a .22 would fit.

She'd have to find a secure place to put it. There was no way that she was going to give Nick an opportunity to sample the massage oil that worked like chloroform!

Danielle smiled in triumph. She was now an official member of the Cartel. She ran her hands over the contents.

"So what was it?" Nick said, coming up behind her.

She sucked in a quick breath. "Oh, Savannah convinced me to join Tender Loving Care with her and her mother. It's like Avon." She smiled up at him.

He shook his head and chuckled. "Women and their products. Sure you're going to have time?"

"Well, they have meetings periodically, and you sell at your leisure."

Nick shrugged. "Have fun. I'll be in the workroom. I want to put the contact sheets together."

"Okay."

He stopped and said over his shoulder, "By the way, you can be my Avon Lady anytime."

She laughed, feeling warm all over just thinking

about all the naughty things they had done the night before. Her body still tingled. Nick did things with ice cubes that should be illegal. Her still-swollen bud pulsed in agreement. She took the case with the intention of putting it on the top shelf of her closet, when the phone rang. She picked it up in the bedroom.

"Hello?"

"You should have received a package," the now familiar voice said.

"Yes, just a little while ago."

"You'll need to come to the brownstone today and get your assignment. Can you be here by noon?"

Danielle stole a quick glance at the digital clock. "Yes, sure."

"I'll see you at noon. I was right, wasn't I?"

"Right?"

"Yes, about him coming back."

The call disconnected.

Danielle left Nick at the apartment, busily working on the contact sheets from the photo shoots. She headed over to the brownstone. It took the recollection of all of her driver-education classes to keep her from breaking the speed limit. She made it uptown in ten minutes; then it took her another ten minutes to find a parking space.

She took a quick look at the spa across the street. Several men were coming in and out, but thankfully none of them were Bernard. That whole thing with Bernard and Nick, and now Bernard was marrying Claudia—it was all a little much. Nick told her that he'd spent the evening with the man. Bernard just seemed to be everywhere with everyone.

She wasn't sure why it bothered her so much. It just did. She rang the ground-floor bell and was expecting to see Margaret answer the door as usual, but to her surprise it was Claudia.

She greeted Danielle with a big hug. "Hello, sweetheart. Come on in. Congratulations," she added and gently squeezed her arm. "Welcome to the family."

"Thanks. I hear congratulations are in order for you," she said, looking Claudia over and seeing that she was as fashionable as ever in an aqua-blue shirtdress, with a split along the left side, complemented by a pair of cream sling backs. And her short, sleek haircut was perfect as always.

Claudia beamed. "Isn't it exciting! I am so happy."

Danielle leaned down and brushed her cheek with a light kiss. "You deserve it."

Claudia's exuberant expression slowly evaporated. She lowered her gaze. "Anna doesn't think so."

"Of course she does. Why would you say that?"

"I know my daughter. I could hear it in her voice."

Danielle took a short breath. How could she tell her that she had her own reservations about Bernard? He seemed to be too good to be true, everyone's best friend. "Savannah will come around. She loves you and wants you to be happy." She hugged Claudia around her shoulders. "You'll see."

Claudia pressed her lips together and nodded. "Well, come on. You don't want to keep Jean waiting."

"Will I see you before I go?"

"I'll be down in the front room working on some reports."

"Okay. And, Claudia, don't worry about Savannah. Promise?"

"Promise," she said, not at all convincingly.

Danielle tapped on Jean's door.

"Come in, Danielle."

This lady really gave her the willies. She came in and closed the door behind her.

"Please have a seat. We have a lot to go over, and I want you to be clear about everything before you leave."

"This is the envelope that was given to Savannah. As you can see, it still has the seal on it. The reason being that once the envelope is opened, the information dissolves within the hour."

Danielle wanted to laugh. It sounded like something Mr. Phelps would say to one of his *Mission: Impossible* agents. But she was sure that Jean wouldn't appreciate the humor.

"I'm not sure how much Savannah may or may not have told you, but the assignment is to infiltrate an elite identity theft ring. They have amassed a fortune by taking over the lives of unsuspecting people. They've gained property, bank accounts, credit cards. We know that their base is in New York, but we need them to lead us to the ringleaders." She paused, folded her hands and looked Danielle hard in the eyes. "There's one catch. This assignment is twofold, the government's half and ours."

"Ours?"

"Several of the victims have come to me personally.

They…can't go to the authorities. They can't afford to have their backgrounds investigated should this hit the news. Am I clear?"

"Y-yes."

"Good." She slid the envelope across the table. "The list is inside, with all of the information you need to get started." She went into her desk drawer and pulled out a shiny new PDA. It looked simple enough, but Danielle knew that it would be her lifeline. Jean passed the PDA to Danielle. "The Cartel is at your disposal. I'll expect regular updates. Be sure to review the CD that came with your kit."

"I did, but I will again," she said.

"Any questions?"

"I thought TLC worked within the law. Why are you working with people who don't want to prosecute?"

Jean lifted her chin. "Sometimes in this business we have to do things…that are not sanctioned. And sometimes we do things for friends." She held Danielle's gaze. "If you have any reservations, now is the time to tell me."

Danielle looked at the envelope and the PDA, then at Jean. She thought about Nick.

"I can do this," she said finally.

"Good." Jean stood up. "Good luck."

"Thank you." She got up, took the envelope and PDA and put them in her oversize purse, then turned and walked out.

When she got down to the first floor, Claudia was in the sitting room, going over a stack of papers. She looked up when Danielle crossed the doorway.

"All done?"

"Yep." She joined Claudia on the antique lounge chair. Now that she'd officially gotten the assignment, she felt she could broach the question that had been plaguing her. "Claudia, I have to ask you... I mean, I know that Bernard goes to the spa across the street. He's somehow teamed up with Nick. How do you keep him from finding out about this place?"

Claudia's glance darted away for an instant. "Bernard is very understanding. And I keep up with his schedule and plan my activities accordingly."

Danielle absorbed the information. "I guess it will be a bit easier now," Danielle said, "but when I was leaving here the other night, I ran right into Nick, and I'd seen Bernard earlier. I was a nervous wreck."

"I know, Savannah told me. You'll simply have to be careful, Dani. They must never know."

Danielle nodded. "Well, thanks for the advice. I need to get going. Nick will be wondering what happened to me."

"You take care, sweetheart," Claudia said, walking Danielle to the door. "And you know if you need anything, I'm here to help in any way that I can."

"Thanks." She gave a shaky smile. "I'm going to need it."

Danielle headed back home, eager to review the contents of the envelope. Identity theft, she thought. Of all the assignments to get, she landed the one thing she'd been battling with her entire life—*identity*.

Although hers hadn't been "stolen," she'd always battled with who she was. But even more pressing in her mind was who the people were who couldn't go to the police.

Curiosity was gnawing at her, but she knew that she had a short window to review the material before the ink dissolved. She couldn't risk pulling over and tearing the envelope open before she was someplace private and quiet.

Then she thought about the library on 136th Street. She could have all the privacy and quiet she needed. She made the turn and drove toward Adam Clayton Powell Jr. Boulevard and 136th Street.

She parked in the lot across the street and hopped out. Once inside, she found one of the computer tables that also had Internet access. Her privacy was afforded by the two short partitions on either side of the desk where she sat.

Her fingers shook as she took the envelope from her bag. She looked around, took a deep breath and lifted the seal. Slowly she pulled the pages out of the envelope.

For the next hour she went over the material. Each of the eight pages highlighted the victims, providing details of all their personal information and the degree to which they'd been violated. The names weren't familiar, but the level to which they'd been taken advantage of was mind-boggling.

Their computers had been hacked and all of their personal information accessed: passwords, banking information and credit-card numbers. In two of the cases, victims reported that though they'd never been to the Caribbean or to Europe, there were massive charges to their credit cards to prove they'd traveled there, along with airline manifest lists showing that they'd been on flights they'd never taken. Which meant that not only their finances were accessed, but also *who* they were. Somewhere, these people were actually posing as the victims, complete with driver's licenses, birth certificates and passports.

Danielle keyed all the victims' names into her PDA, along with contact information, then saved it with a pass code, as she'd been instructed. Although all the information in her PDA was encrypted, it didn't hurt to take that one extra step, Jasmine had advised during her training.

The most disturbing were the victims who refused to go to the authorities. And when it registered who they were, Danielle immediately knew why.

One was Doris and Richard Matlock. He was the CEO of Empress Oil, one of the largest distributors of oil in the United States, with connections in the Middle East.

The other was Leslie Davenport, head of the Davenport Foundation, which was responsible for overseeing more than fifty charity and nonprofit organizations in New York.

Danielle leaned back in the chair, stunned. This was major. When she'd read stories about identity theft, she'd never comprehended the magnitude of how it could devastate people's lives. It was disturbing that people wanted to hide the fact that they'd been duped.

She put those pages aside and began to go over the information that had been gathered to date. It was clear that the central headquarters was headed by someone inside New York City and that there were several levels of people involved—from the top man or woman to the actual thieves themselves. It was also clear that at some point the victims must have come in contact with the thieves either in their daily lives or through business.

There was a short list of possible places to start. Whoever was behind this was highly skilled technologically and could move in and out of elite circles without being questioned. What struck her as most chilling was that these people, whoever they were, actually masqueraded as the victims in public places and were able to get away with it.

She made some additional notes in her PDA, then continued to read the backup information.

There was a paragraph about a man who'd been on the watch list for about six months, but they could never tie him to anything. They believed he was high up in the chain of command and were certain that the name he was using was false. *Bernard Hassell.*

Danielle stopped breathing. She blinked several times, rubbed her eyes and read the name again. It had to be wrong, she thought, as her head began to pound. "There must be a million Bernard Hassells," she sputtered nervously.

She read on and the information gave her a link to a photograph. With shaky fingers she picked up her PDA and after several attempts was able to finally key in the link information. Her heart pounded and her stomach rose and fell as she waited for the image to appear. She was sure that there was some kind of mistake and her own vivid imagination was simply in overdrive. To think that the Bernard she knew and the one in this file were the same person was ridiculous.

The image began to unfold on the sixteen-inch-wide screen.

Danielle's loud gasp turned several curious heads in

her direction. The last thing she needed was to draw attention to herself. She focused on the images and information on the screen.

She covered her mouth in shocked disbelief. Bernard Hassell, Claudia's fiancé, Savannah's potential stepfather and now Nick's new buddy, stared back at her.

Chapter 10

Danielle sat there unable to move. She sat there for so long—staring at the image and trying to slow down her racing thoughts—that when she pulled herself together, she noticed that the ink on the pages was beginning to lighten. The first page was already blank.

She didn't even care. She felt ill. What was she going to do? How in good conscience could she not tell Claudia? Or Savannah or Nick?

But what if the information was wrong? she reasoned. That was possible. Maybe it only appeared that Bernard was someone involved. Innocent people are implicated in things all the time.

Her gut told her something else entirely. And that was that Jean Armstrong didn't make mistakes—not a mistake like this one—which meant that she already knew about Claudia and Bernard…like she knew about everything.

What really made her stomach turn was the fact that Jean had planned to give this assignment to Savannah. How was she supposed to handle this information when it related to her own mother?

My God, Jean, what kind of bitch are you?

Anger flushed through her system. Now they were messing with her friends, her surrogate family. That made it all very personal.

She snatched up the now blank pages, stuffed them into her bag, turned off her PDA and dropped it inside as well. All she could see was red, and she knew she needed to get to her car and calm down so that she could think and work out a plan.

The trouble was, as much as Jean told her that the Cartel resources were available to her and she could always use one of the members for assistance, that, too, was a bunch of crap. How? How could she possibly bring in any of the members on something so sensitive? She'd never want any of them to know that Claudia was involved with someone who was being investigated in a major series of crimes.

After sliding into the driver's seat, she slammed her fist against the steering wheel, but she was so angry she barely registered the shock of pain that jetted up her arm.

Danielle lowered her head onto the wheel and took in long, deep breaths. She had to be clearheaded. She couldn't overreact and allow her feelings to make mistakes for her.

She looked up. First things first—go home to her man. Then she'd take one step at a time.

* * *

When she got back to her apartment, Nick was on his way out.

"Hey, babe. I'm heading out for a few." He slung his knapsack over his right shoulder. He turned and actually focused on her. His brow wrinkled. "You okay? You look like you ate something bad." He walked over to her.

"I'm fine." She smiled. "I was hoping we could spend the afternoon together," she said, feeling the need to be with and hold on to something real.

"Wow. I figured you'd be gone for a while. I decided to get a jump on the JCPenney project. I'm going with Mark to scout out some locations." He cupped her chin. "I promise, I'll be back as soon as I can." He leaned down and kissed her, giving her just a little bit of tongue.

Danielle suddenly clung to him, wrapping her arms tightly around his neck. She buried her face in the hollow of his neck and inhaled his scent.

"I swear, I won't be more than two hours," he said lightly. He leaned back, looked down at her and lifted her chin with the tip of his finger. His eyes ran back and forth across her face. "Then I'm all yours, okay?"

She nodded, not daring to speak over the knot in her throat.

"Be back before you know it." He pecked her lips one last time, then headed out.

Danielle released a long, heavy sigh and aimlessly wandered through the apartment, trying to line up her thoughts. She finally plopped down on the living-room couch, her long legs splayed out in front of her. She folded her arms across her stomach and stared across the room at a piece of art by Budson, an Atlanta-based artist, that hung on the far wall.

It was the photograph of a man and woman intertwined on what looked like a couch. But their bodies were so intricately coupled that it was hard to determine where one began and the other ended.

How appropriate that she would have a picture where the identities in the portrait were marred by illusion.

There'd been moments on the drive home that she'd begun to believe she was the wrong person for this assignment. But in examining the portrait and her life, she thought, who better than she to uncover those who pretend to be something they aren't?

Hadn't she been pretending all her life, allowing her looks—her silky hair and exotic features—to gain her access to people and places she wouldn't have otherwise had access to? It was so much easier in life to go through the open doors rather than having to knock them down. She'd never had to stand up for a cause in her life. She didn't have to. Those ugly things in the world didn't apply to her. She was above it all, moving through life in that privileged circle of acceptance. She'd gotten so good at it that she'd forgotten she wasn't really one of the chosen ones. That was until she looked at a family portrait, the picture of her father, dark as a moonless night and her mother light as a brand-new day, with ink-colored hair that met the rise of her behind.

For years the stares from strangers made her secretly ashamed of her father's blackness, his coarse hair, wide nose and thick lips. And she hated the taunts her classmates tossed at her about her father's strong ethnic features.

Every guy she'd dated since high school had been white or Hispanic or a light-skinned black with "good hair." All practices and beliefs that had been unconsciously ingrained in her from her grandmother—things she'd been unable to shake all these years.

That was the ugliness that stalked her thoughts and emotions day in and day out. She rested her head back against the cushion of the couch and closed her eyes. It was the shadow that hovered around her heart when it came to Nick and her feelings for him.

Was she with him because he fit the image she'd imposed on herself years ago, or did she really care for him? Or worse, did she care for him only because of his appearance and not for who he was?

She hadn't seen her parents in years, and she felt the always present ache in her heart. Only her closest friends—Mia and Savannah—even knew who her parents were.

In college, the girls had always teased her about her choice in men, dating only the white or pretty boys. But to this day, neither Mia nor Savannah knew the terror that lurked in her heart about one day settling down and having a child that looked like her dad. A child who would grow up in a world that valued looks over substance. A child who would be teased by classmates and would begin to devalue themselves, and the vicious cycle would continue.

She'd never forget the time she was walking into the apartment building where they lived when she was about twelve. The downstairs neighbors were in the hallway talking when she came in from school.

"Hi, Mrs. Walker, Ms. Daisy."

"Hi. Looking beautiful as always," Mrs. Walker said.

"Had a good day at school?" Ms. Daisy asked.

"Yep." She started up the steps and was on the next landing putting her key in the door to her apartment when their voices floated up to her.

"Her father is going to have some time keeping the boys away when she gets to dating age," Danielle heard Mrs. Walker say.

"All he has to do is show that ugly black face and scare them away!"

They laughed as if that was the best joke.

"I swear that child's mama must have been drunk when she laid down with that man."

"Chile is lucky she looks like her mama…"

And she had been "lucky" that she looked like her mother. It had given her a free pass in life. She never had to do much more than smile. Even her business was an outgrowth of all the self-hatred that she had about herself and who she was. What did she choose for a career? Photographing beautiful people and beautiful clothes, creating images that no one could ever live up to.

Knowing that about herself made her sick. She might be able to deceive others but never herself. The truth was evident each time she looked in the mirror. She was a fake. Just like the people she had to go after. She had to do this. She had to, not only for the victims but for herself.

Danielle sniffed hard and realized she was crying. She swiped away at the tears with the back of her hand just as the phone rang, and went to the kitchen to get it. She cleared her throat.

"Hello."

"You could sound more enthused to hear from me!"

Danielle's sour mood quickly elevated.

"Mia! Girl, how are you? Are you home?"

"On my way. I just landed at JFK. We're pulling up to the gate."

Suddenly Danielle felt as if she would burst into tears. "It's so good to hear your voice," she said, even as hers cracked with emotion.

"Dani, what's wrong? I know you didn't miss me that much."

Mia was always able to read her like a book. She sniffed. "Just can't wait to see you." She paused. "I need someone to talk to." Tears spilled down her cheeks.

"I have a car waiting for me. I'm going to swing by your place on the way home. It sounds like you need one of my famous meals."

Danielle laughed lightly through her tears. "Thanks."

"Give Savannah a call and tell her to meet us when she gets off work."

"No!"

"Why? What's up? Did you and Anna have a falling out?"

Danielle swallowed. "No. It's nothing like that. It's— it's just the things I need to say to you. I can't have Savannah hear them."

"Oh" was all Mia could initially manage. "Whatever it is, we'll work it out, sweetie. Promise. Now put on something fierce and I'll see you soon."

"Thanks, Mia."

"Hey, what are friends for?"

The call disconnected.

Exactly, Danielle thought. What are friends for if not to have each other's back? She'd work this out. One way or the other.

Chapter 11

On the ride from Danielle's apartment to Mia's co-op, Mia filled Danielle's ear with tales from her trip, the exciting people she'd met and the killer client list she'd built.

Mia Turner's success was hinged on who she knew. And in New York, Mia knew everyone. As an event planner for major corporations and moneybag clients, she had to know the best restaurants, chefs, vacation spots, airlines, designers—everyone who was anyone and all of their assistants. Mia was on a first-name basis with virtually every secretary in the city. It always pays to get in good with the secretaries and personal assistants, she'd often said. They know everything and will be the ones to get you behind closed doors when no one else can.

Nothing could have been more true. Mia's connections had garnered the trio the prime tables in restaurants, best seats at premieres and countless free trips to exotic resorts and spas.

She may be a bit anal at times with her quirks about perfection and time, Danielle thought, but she more than made up for it with her giving nature.

"Wow, it's good to be home," Mia enthused once the key turned the lock and the door swung open. She dropped her bags in the hallway and strolled through her space, spinning around in a circle—for a moment Danielle thought Mia might do that Mary Tyler Moore move and throw her hat up in the air.

Instead, Mia collapsed into a champagne-colored armchair and kicked off her shoes.

"I'm not sure what's in the fridge. Steve isn't much of a cook or shopper," she said with a soft smile framing her full mouth.

"Did you call him to let him know you were back?"

"Yep. He said he would try to get home early. He and Blake were working on a new project, and they had a late meeting set up." She angled her head to the side. "You wanna talk or you wanna eat?"

Danielle smiled. "Both."

Mia pushed herself up from the chair and grabbed Danielle's hand. "Come on and tell me all about it."

As Danielle washed romaine lettuce and diced cucumbers and tomatoes, Mia seasoned a fresh piece of salmon to get it ready for baking.

Danielle talked as she worked, bringing Mia up-to-the-minute information on what she'd been assigned to do, and the ambivalence she felt in doing it.

"Dayum," Mia murmured. "This would kill Claudia—if it's true," she qualified.

"I know. But like I've been saying, there's been something bugging me about Bernard since the day he showed up at my apartment with Nick."

"Right. I remember." She turned and glanced at Danielle over her shoulder. "Sorry I just tossed your concerns off."

Danielle waved off the apology. "No need to apologize. You didn't know and neither did I. But now we do."

"Wow, suppose Bernard is trying to get close to Nick to steal his identity or yours."

Danielle chuckled at that. "I think he would really be pissed off if he did. I have about ten dollars more than zero."

"Chile, please. I know you are doing well."

"I know, but not the kind of *well* that these people are interested in. You should see the list and what's been taken from them. Scary."

Mia put the tray with the salmon in the oven, rinsed her hands and joined Danielle at the kitchen table. She dried her hands on a paper towel, rolled it into a ball and set it on the center of the table.

"So what's your plan?" Mia asked.

"I'm figuring the first thing I need to do is work with what I know. And the only one that I know in this scenario is Bernard."

"Makes sense," Mia said. She played with the rolled-up paper towel for a moment, hoping that, given some breathing room, Danielle would spill the rest on her own. Several moments passed. "Okay, now that we have all that nasty spy business out of the way, you want to tell me what's really bothering you? I could hear it in your voice, and I know it's not about the case, especially if you didn't want Savannah to be here."

Danielle glanced away; she didn't want Mia to see the self-hatred that hung in her eyes or the guilt that colored her life.

"Whatever it is, talking about it will help. It always does," she said gently. "Did something happen between you and Savannah?"

Danielle shook her head. "No. Nothing like that." She swallowed, her throat feeling thick and tight. She reached for the glass of spring water and took a long swallow. Slowly she lowered the glass.

"There are things…that you don't know about me, things that I'm ashamed of."

"Ashamed of? Like what? We all have something about ourselves that we don't like. How bad could it be?"

"Ashamed of who I am," she said in a monotone. She looked straight at Mia.

Mia frowned in confusion. "What do you mean?"

Danielle looked away, beyond Mia, back to a time in her life that she'd never wanted to revisit but which had tainted every move she'd made ever since.

She was a senior in college and madly in love with Michael Fleming, a grad student in the art department. Michael was one of the beautiful people. Everything about him was perfect, from the shape of his eyes and the sweep of his thick brows to the body of Adonis and the pinch of cinnamon on his skin, giving him the appearance of a year-round tan. Not only was Michael heavenly to look at, but he was wealthy to boot. His father, Jackson Fleming, made his mint with hotels, running one of the most successful privately owned hotel chains in the country. He started out with a ten-room motel in Silver Springs, Maryland, which grew to fifteen hotels and resorts throughout the United States. Fleming Hotel and Resorts were synonymous with class and money.

As the only child, Michael would inherit it all as long as he toed daddy's line: went to school, got his master's and brought home the perfect wife to carry on the Fleming legacy.

Danielle was completely captivated by Michael. He took her places she'd only dreamed of, such as a spur-of-the-moment weekend in Paris, skiing in Aspen or dinner on his father's yacht. And they would always end their evenings making love.

Michael was as gifted in bed as he was in looks and stature. She'd been with a few men before him but none who could satisfy her. All along she'd been faking it, not wanting to hurt anyone's feelings, but with Michael it was real and so damned good she knew she was addicted. She couldn't get enough of him, and they made love every chance they got.

Michael was exceptionally virile one particular night. They'd just come home from an art gallery opening when they tumbled into Danielle's tiny one-bedroom apartment in lower Manhattan, better known as Alphabet City. Danielle lived on Avenue C in a five-story walk-up. She was on the third floor.

She turned the key in the lock, and the instant the door opened, Michael swept her up in his arms and took her to the bedroom. He plopped her down on the bed even as he was taking off his pristine white shirt, tossing it to the floor.

Danielle scrambled out of her peasant skirt and shirred blouse, her heart puttering like crazy from seeing the hot look in his eyes.

Before she knew what was happening, Michael was all over her. There didn't seem to be a spot on her body that he didn't pay homage to.

The force of his entry pinned her to the mattress and trapped the strangled cry of exquisite pleasure in her throat. He rode her like a man who'd lost his way in the dark, had been starved, afraid, lonely and had suddenly seen daylight—and everything he'd ever wanted was only a stroke away—and he moved toward it as hard and as fast as he could.

Danielle felt the incredible hardness of him fill every square inch of her, and she knew that at any moment Michael would find his release and she wanted to be there with him.

He grabbed her, wrapping his arms around her body. She locked her ankles behind his back, sealing them together.

Michael's heartbeat slammed against Danielle's breasts. The veins in his neck bulged as sweat dripped from his forehead down the valley of her chest.

He groaned, so deep and hard as he pushed inside her to the hilt.

"Marry me," he said on a ragged breath.

Danielle's mind spun.

He pounded into her again. "Marry…me."

Her body was on fire. She was searing with wet, hot need. His thrusts sent shards of electricity racing through her limbs, short-circuiting her brain.

"Say yes," he demanded. He ground his hips against her, and an explosion of lights erupted behind her eyelids. Her body shook as wave after wave of satisfaction coursed through her. "Say it," he urged as he leaned down, took a nipple into his mouth and pushed her completely over the edge.

"Yes!" she screamed at the moment that Michael emptied himself into her.

"Did you mean that?" she asked a bit later as they lay entwined with each other on the damp and twisted sheets.

He pushed her hair away from her face and looked into her uncertain eyes.

"Of course I meant it. I love you. I'm crazy about you and I want to spend the rest of my life with you." He brushed her slightly swollen lips with the tip of his thumb. "Do you feel the same way about me?"

She nodded vigorously, too overcome to speak. This was more than she could have ever hoped to have happen to her. Michael Fleming was considered one of the greatest catches of his generation. And he was hers. She was going to be Mrs. Michael Fleming. It must be a dream.

For the next two weeks, whenever they had free time, they were shopping for the perfect engagement ring.

They finally found what they were looking for in a specialty diamond shop on Fifth Avenue in Manhattan. It was a marquis diamond surrounded by eight baguettes and set in platinum.

"Oh, Michael, it's incredible."

"Just like you." He kissed her tenderly. "We'll take it," Michael said to the dealer before taking her mouth again.

"This feels like some kind of dream," she whispered.

"If it is, I never want to wake up."

But she did wake up, much sooner than she would have wanted.

She'd met Michael's parents on several occasions; now it was her turn to introduce her parents to them. In the days leading up to the lunch she'd planned for her parents and Michael's parents, she'd wondered why she'd never discussed her parentage and her own mixed ethnicity with Michael. It just wasn't something that came up in everyday conversation. She should have and could have avoided the humiliation that ensued.

But she hadn't, and now here she was in the middle of Cipriani's, with the wall of politeness so thick that none of the six people sitting at the table could speak for fear of saying what was really on their minds and causing the thin thread of civility to snap.

When Michael's mother was introduced to Danielle's father, her mouth dropped open. From some deep reserve of upbringing, she forced a smile, and maneuvered herself in such a way that she sat down before she had to shake his outstretched hand.

Mr. Fleming cleared his throat after the waiter

came and placed the menus on the table. "So where did you two meet?"

Danielle's mother spoke up. "We both worked for the board of education."

"Maintenance?" Mrs. Fleming asked. "I mean, not teachers."

"I'm a science teacher and my wife teaches math."

"How interesting," Mrs. Fleming said. "Affirmative action is such a wonderful thing. Isn't it, dear," she said to her husband.

Inwardly, Danielle grew smaller and smaller, imagining what was going through Mr. and Mrs. Fleming's minds, seeing the pain on her mother's and father's faces and not caring. All she wanted was for the afternoon to be over.

"I'm going to, uh, spend the night with my folks out on Long Island tonight," Michael said, pulling her aside after the excruciatingly long two-hour lunch. His parents had already said their goodbyes, paid the check and were outside. But not before pulling Michael off to the side to speak with him privately.

Danielle's heart was in her throat. She gripped his hands, her diamond flashing in the afternoon sun. "Michael…"

"I have to go. I'll call you later on tonight." He turned without another word and walked out.

"He seems like a very nice young man," her mother said, slowly rising from her seat.

Danielle turned to her mother and father, simple, ordinary, decent people whom she knew loved her without question and she wished that they would disappear.

"I've got to get home. I have a test in the morning." She couldn't look them in the eye.

"They seem like nice enough people," her father said, speaking for the first time in a while. "But they are the kind of people who look at you from the outside. It wouldn't matter what you were made of. And I'm sorry to say, their son is no different."

"What do you know? What do you know about anything?" She leaped up from her seat, knocking a teacup to the floor. "I hate you. Both of you. You've ruined everything." She spun away and ran out into the street and kept on running until she was out of breath and soaking wet with perspiration. She stopped on a corner, hailed a cab and went home, fully expecting a message from Michael.

"But he didn't call," Danielle said, still trapped in time. "Not that night or the next. I didn't hear from him for about a week. Finally I couldn't take it anymore and went looking for him in every classroom on his campus. I finally found him, and he acted like he didn't know me."

"Talk to me, Mike. This is me, Danielle, the woman you swore to love, the woman you gave this to," she had pleaded. She held out her hand, and the diamond sparkled in the sunlight.

"It's best if we…don't see each other, Danielle," he said coldly, as if he were reading a laundry list of chores.

The world seemed to stand still. What he said didn't make any sense. "What…are you saying?" She grabbed his arm. "You love me! What do you mean? We're supposed to get married."

"Don't do this, Dani." He tried to pull away.

"Do what? Ask you to explain why you're doing this? Tell me, dammit!"

"Fine! There's no way that I can marry you and take the chance on…on having a child that…looks like your father."

The air was sucked out of her lungs. The pulse in her temples pounded, blurring her vision. When the world around her came back into focus, Michael was halfway across campus.

"Dani, I'm so sorry." Mia reached across the table to cover her hand. "He was a bastard. It's his loss."

Tears fell in a steady stream down her face. She swiped them away with the back of her hand but they were immediately replaced.

"About a month later I found out I was pregnant."

Mia squeezed her hand a bit tighter.

"I don't know if it was fate or fortune. Before I could digest what I was going to do, I had a miscarriage."

Mia was speechless. This was an entire era of her friend's life that she knew nothing about.

Danielle sniffed hard. "It was one thing for me to endure harsh criticism and ugly words about my parents from other people, but for them to be voiced by someone I believed myself to be in love with only validated the ugliness of it all."

"Dani, that was a long time ago. You're all grown up, a different person."

"That's just it, I'm not different. At least I'm not sure if I am. That day did something to me. It stole a piece of me. I haven't dared allowed myself to feel that way again about anyone. I didn't want to take the chance…"

"Until Nick?"

Danielle nodded. "But what terrifies me is I don't know if the way I feel about him is real or if it's simply easy because of how he looks—the pretty boy—the image I've worked out in my mind that is right for me. And what if he met my parents? It would kill me if he reacted the way Michael did. I couldn't take it."

Mia suddenly stood and Danielle was sure she'd gone too far, opened up a door that couldn't be closed. Now she'd lost her friend.

Mia crossed the room and went to the sink. She kept her back to Danielle.

"Dani, all of us have crap about ourselves that we don't like. We do things in life that we are not proud of." She turned to face her and leaned back against the sink as she spoke. "But what separates us from the four-legged creatures is our conscience and our ability to think things through and change the things that are wrong.

"Nick loves you. And I believe that you love him, too—for all the right reasons. But at some point you are going to have to let go of the past so that you can live for the now and move into the future. You'll never know the kind of man Nick is or the kind of woman you are until you give him the chance to show you. You've got to trust his love for you, or you'll never find happiness with him or anyone."

Danielle's smile was wobbly at best. "For someone who just found Mr. Right, you sure have a lot of good advice."

"I've been practicing."

* * *

By the time Danielle returned to her apartment, she was feeling much better. Mia had a way of turning lemons into lemonade, even if the lemons were rotten.

As much as she dreaded the inevitable, at some point she was going to have to be totally honest with Nick about everything. Well…almost everything.

She sauntered in, full of purpose, and was secretly glad that Nick hadn't gotten back yet. The scouting must have taken longer than he thought. She headed for the bedroom and was going to use her time alone to do some investigating. But she had no intention of being caught off guard when Nick could walk through the door at any moment. She called him on his cell phone. It rang three times before he picked up.

"Hey, babe. Actually we finished up about an hour ago," Nick said. "But I decided to run over to the gym. And guess who I ran into? Bernard. So we're gonna hang out for a bit and then I'll be home. See you soon. Okay?"

He stuck his cell back in its case on his hip, smiling as he did so.

"That must have been your lady love," Bernard said, coming up to Nick, a towel draped around his neck. He mopped his face with the tail of the towel.

"That transparent, huh?"

"It's a vibe and a look in the eye. Nothing wrong with that. Let's other ladies know that you're taken. Cuts down on a lot of drama," he said with a chuckle.

"Yeah, you're probably right."

They walked toward the treadmill.

"Have you and Claudia set a date yet?"

"I'd prefer sooner rather than later, something small and intimate. But Claudia is not hearing that. She wants the whole package."

"Well, from what I hear, weddings are all about the women anyway. The guys are just told where to show up and when."

Both men laughed.

"You're absolutely right," Bernard said.

"You ever been married before?" Nick asked.

"No."

"Any reason?"

Bernard turned on his machine, and the track beneath his feet began to move. Nick followed suit.

"Never found the right woman who could deal with my long hours and weeks of being away from home."

"Oh." Nick pushed up the dial to heighten the incline. "I don't think I've ever asked you what you do…or did." He blew out slowly through his mouth and inhaled deeply.

"Army, for a lot of years."

"Really," he said, beginning to feel the burn in his upper thighs. "How many?"

"I retired after twenty-five years," he said, still not breaking a sweat.

"Long time. You into anything now?"

Bernard turned his head to look at Nick. "Pretty much whatever I want."

Nick chuckled. "What a life."

Although Mia could not "officially" be involved, she'd promised Danielle she'd make some discreet inquiries regarding Bernard. It would be up to Danielle, however, to get some basics.

Her kit came equipped with hacking software that Jasmine had gleefully showed her how to use. She went to the closet and took the kit down from the top shelf.

Taking it to the bed, she opened the top and took out an innocuous-looking compact. She opened it and pried behind the mirror to reveal a small computer disk. The disk contained six hacking programs that would gain her access to the three major credit-card companies, Department of Health, phone company, Department of Motor Vehicles, Social Security Administration and Internal Revenue Service.

She put the disk into her laptop. First she accessed the Department of Health database, entered Bernard's approximate age and keyed in his name. The list was too long to even bother with. From there she tried the phone company, and as bizarre as it was, there wasn't one listing in Manhattan for Bernard Hassell. He didn't even show up in the unlisted directory. Maybe he used only a cell phone, like many people did these days. But it was still curious. She tried the credit-card companies, the IRS and the Department of Motor Vehicles. Either she came up blank, more often than not, or the profiles didn't match.

Frustrated, Danielle ejected the disk and returned it to its hiding place. She was going to need more concrete information to go on in order to narrow her search. But the more she thought about it, the more concerned she became. Something wasn't right.

Bernard wasn't the only piece of the puzzle, however. There were the victims she needed to concentrate on to find out who had stolen their identities.

She began by plugging the names, one by one, into

the PDA while waiting for the Wi-Fi to connect with the main terminal at the brownstone. Within moments she had access to their computers.

She made notes and planned to give the list to Mia to see if she knew or had knowledge of anyone on it.

Danielle shut down the computer and turned off the PDA. At least now she didn't feel so helpless. She was doing something. Somehow she had to get behind the wall that Bernard Hassell had built around himself. There had to be an opening somewhere. What she needed was some inside information. And since she couldn't very well ask the astute Claudia, the next likely candidate was Nick.

Chapter 12

"So you and Bernard are getting to be pretty good friends," Danielle mentioned casually as they sat on the couch watching Jay Leno on *The Tonight Show*.

"He's a really decent guy," Nick said. "I like him."

"He must be nice for Claudia to decide to marry him."

"True," he said absentmindedly then tossed his head back and laughed at one of Jay's barbs about dumb criminals.

"Where is he from?"

"Who?"

"Bernard."

"Oh, uh, I think he told me he was originally from D.C."

She filed that bit of information away. "Is he working now or retired?"

He played with a lock of her hair while he listened to the rest of the "Headlines." It was his favorite portion of the show.

Danielle gently nudged him in the ribs.

"Ouch, what did I do?"

"I'm talking to you, and you're not even paying me any attention."

"I'm sorry, what did you say?"

A commercial was on, so she had his full attention.

"I was asking you what Bernard does for a living or if he's retired?"

"Oh. Retired from the army. Did twenty-five years."

"Hmm, impressive." There had to be some information on him if he'd been in the army. "He lives in Manhattan, right?"

"Yeah. Why are you so interested in Bernard all of a sudden?"

Her stomach clenched. She shrugged. "No special interest. You know all of my friends, and since he seems to be one of yours now and is going to marry my best friend's mother, I want to get an idea of who he is. That's all."

"Well, I mean, he's a nice guy. Good listener, funny, likes sports and working out in the gym. What else is there?" He turned to her and grinned. "Satisfied, Sherlock?"

"Very funny." She settled down into his embrace and pretended to focus on the rest of the show, but her mind was a million miles away.

The following morning they were greeted by dark skies and torrents of rain. According to the forecast the rest of the day wouldn't be much better.

Nick was in the kitchen scrambling some eggs when Danielle joined him, her face still soft from sleep.

"Mornin'."

"Hi," she said over a yawn and plopped down at the table. "Smells good."

"Want me to fix you a plate?"

"No, coffee is good."

"Oh, I turned in my keys to my place yesterday and paid them for the last month's rent. So I guess you're stuck with me for real."

She laughed lightly in response. "Looks that way. But who's complaining." She winked at him.

As she sat there allowing her head to clear, she watched Nick as he worked. He was a wonderful man in every way. Any woman would be lucky to have him. He was handsome, sexy, an unselfish lover, funny and talented. Not to mention a great cook.

So she asked herself again, why couldn't she commit? Why couldn't she tell him that she loved him? Why? The question constantly reverberated in her head.

She knew Nick would move mountains to make her happy. Was she willing to do the same? She sighed deeply. They'd only been a couple for less than a year, although they'd worked together for much longer than that.

She'd been reluctant to move out of the safety of a coworker relationship into a personal one. But Nick wouldn't be dissuaded.

"I knew you were the one for me the day you hired me," he'd confessed to her one night over dinner during the early days of their romance.

She grinned. "Is that so?"

"For real."

"How did you know?"

"When I stepped into the studio and caught a glimpse of you behind the camera doing your thing, something happened to me inside. I know it sounds corny but it's true. Then after I got to talk to you and you hired me on the team, it was eating me up inside to be so close to you and not be able to do anything about it."

"I've broken every rule in the 'employer's handbook' by going out with you."

"I know. You risked a lot. And I'm going to prove to you that you didn't make a mistake."

And he had. There wasn't a day that went by that Nick didn't try to show her how much he cared, from keeping their relationship out of the spotlight at work to fixing dinner, running her bath and most recently giving up his apartment.

He'd turned his heart and his life over to her, but she didn't seem able to do the same. And as much as he loved her, she wasn't sure how long her lack of indecisiveness with regard to their relationship could go on without him deciding to leave.

He brought his plate of eggs to the table, then the pot of coffee. He filled her mug and sat down.

"I already called the crew to cancel for today. Even if the rain stops, there's no way we can get any decent shots."

She nodded in agreement and took a sip of her coffee. "It worked out anyway. I totally forgot I have an appointment at the Preston Studio this afternoon. I need to go over their schedule to coordinate the photography time."

"Well, while you're gone I'll get with the crew and the models to reschedule. We should have had a plan B in place for something just like this—an alternative indoor location."

"We usually do. I guess it just slipped under the radar."

"We'll plan better next time. Did you rest well?"

"Yes, I think so. Why?"

"You were mumbling in your sleep last night."

Her nerves tightened. "Really? Did I say anything interesting?"

"Got me. Sounded like you were talking about a *cartel.*" He chuckled and she almost strangled on her coffee. "Must have been the aftereffects of something you watched on TV." He forked a mouthful of eggs and chewed slowly.

"Yeah, I guess," she muttered.

He finished his eggs and took his plate to the sink. "I'm going to get busy contacting folks and coordinating schedules." He ruffled her hair as he walked by her.

She felt light-headed. *Talking in her sleep.* She never knew she did that, but then again until you sleep with someone every night, who was going to tell you? What if she'd really said something damaging, incriminating? Oh, God. The coffee in her stomach burned.

Danielle arrived at the Michael Preston Studio shortly before two. This time Tasha was waiting for her at the reception desk. She stuck out her hand.

"Good to see you again. Horrible day out. You can drop your umbrella in the stand by the desk."

"Thanks." She took off her light raincoat and gently shook her umbrella before depositing it in the stand, then followed Tasha down the corridor.

"Come right in," she said, holding open the door to her office. "So how have you been?" She walked around the large desk that was covered in swatches of fabric and photographs.

"Busy," Danielle said. "But that's a good thing."

"Please excuse the mess and have a seat at the conference table. It will be much easier to work." Tasha opened a large file cabinet that was built into the wall and extracted an oversize portfolio and brought it to the table. She began flipping through the pages, talking as she did so.

"These are the models that we will use for the collection. But what I'd like you to do is meet with them and get a sense of who they are and how they work. Since everyone is so busy, scheduling is going to be a major undertaking. But I can have one of the assistants take care of that."

"Fine."

"I'm thinking it will take a couple of weeks to pull it all together before we can even get started. But I'm sure we should be ready with everyone in place no later than the second week in June. By that time all of the pieces will be completed."

Danielle was taking notes as Tasha spoke.

"I think I counted fifteen models. Is that right?"

Tasha grinned. "On the money. I'd like to take you on a tour of the showroom. The designers have been working nonstop to get everything ready. Many of the new items are available for viewing."

"Sure." She draped her jacket and purse across her arm and followed Tasha out.

The designs for the most part were typical Michael Preston, clean lines, all-American look. His new collection, however, was in bold colors with mix-and-match pieces that could easily go from a day at the office to a night on the town.

"I love what I'm seeing," Danielle said as they made the rounds through the studio.

"Michael wanted to go in a different direction for the fall but still maintain his signature look. We're all very happy with the results."

"I'm sure the store buyers and the ladies will be as well. I know I can do some great things in shooting this line."

Tasha looked purposefully at Danielle. "That's why we hired you. We only want the best."

Danielle's ego had been suitably stroked by the time she left the showroom. She had her work cut out for her, but she had a great team, she thought as she stepped off the elevator and ran right into the woman she'd met a couple of days earlier.

"Alicia Keys!" the woman joked. "Back again, I see."

"I had a meeting."

"My offer still stands. The pay is great, easy hours."

"I don't think so," Danielle said, stepping around her.

"Well, if you change your mind, my office is on twenty."

Danielle pushed a smile across her mouth and walked to the exit.

What people won't do for money, she thought as she stepped out into the rain. She opened her umbrella and darted and dodged around the flow of human traffic until she reached the garage at the end of the street where her car was parked. And just before she went down the ramp, she glanced up the street and could have sworn she saw Bernard coming out of the building she'd just left.

She tried to get a better look, but there were too many people and umbrellas blocking her view. When her line of sight cleared, he was gone.

Danielle shook her head, trying to convince herself that she couldn't have seen Bernard and even if she had, there was no law that said he couldn't have business there as well.

She slowly descended the ramp, trying to re-create that fleeting moment, but as that woman from the elevator had said, everybody looks like somebody. She shook it off and went to retrieve her car.

Instead of going home, Danielle decided to stop by Mia's office in midtown. She'd just returned from a meeting when Danielle pulled up in front.

"Hey, girl. What a surprise." She buzzed her cheek. "Come on in. You know this is a bad hair day…for some of us," she quipped, having pulled her hair in a safe ponytail, unlike Danielle whose beautiful mane simply flowed full of waves in the dampness. "What brings you to my neck of the woods?" She shook out her umbrella and pushed through the glass door.

"I finished up my meeting at the Preston Studio and took a chance that you might be around."

"Well, come on back to my sanctuary and relax a minute. Grace, any messages?" she asked her assistant as she breezed by. "You remember Danielle, right?" she asked over her shoulder but didn't wait for an answer to either question.

"They're on your desk," Grace called out and waved to Danielle.

Mia opened the door to her office, which was a study in pure class. The winter-white walls were strategically adorned with African art. Low-slung chairs and hard-wood tables dotted the glistening wood floors. A huge flat-screen television was mounted on one wall that faced a fabric couch covered in kente cloth and topped with thick throw pillows.

Her ground-floor office was connected to a forty-story condominium that boasted annual rents in the hundreds of thousands. On any given day you were sure to see several movie stars, models or politicians coming in and out. Mia's rent was outrageous, but the perks were worth it, she'd always said.

"So." Mia tossed her jacket onto the back of a chair. "Spill it. Something is definitely on your mind." She reached into her purse for her glasses, which she refused to wear in public.

Danielle told her about her sighting of Bernard.

Mia frowned, behind the thin frames and thick lenses. "It doesn't actually mean anything. I mean, it might not have even been him."

"I know. But I would bet money that it was." She leaned forward. "I know this is going to sound crazy, but I'm starting to think that maybe he's following me."

"Why in the world would you think that?"

"Maybe it's not just coincidence that he hooked up with Nick and showed up at my apartment, or was going to the spa when I was going to the brownstone, or that he turned up today."

"That is a lot of coincidences, but it doesn't really mean anything. Manhattan isn't half as big as we'd like to believe. I think you're just being paranoid."

"Probably." She was quiet for a minute.

"Have you found out any more information about him?"

Danielle brought her up to date on what she'd pried from Nick.

"I was hoping that maybe you could tap some of your resources and see if you can find out anything about him."

"No problem. I'll get started first thing in the morning. Somebody somewhere has to know something about this guy." Her eyes suddenly widened. "I have an idea. Why don't I arrange one of my little dinner parties…to celebrate Claudia and Bernard's engagement. It would get him out of the house and give you a chance to get in…"

Chapter 13

When Danielle arrived back at her apartment, Nick was on the couch watching a basketball game. She hung up her coat, kicked off her shoes and joined him.

"Hey, babe, how'd everything go today?"

She stretched out beside him, and he slid over to make room. She rested her head on his chest.

"Long and wet."

"Hmm, you really shouldn't put those two words together around me. Gives me all kinds of ideas," he teased, kissing her on top of her head.

"You're terrible." She playfully swatted his arm. "Who's winning?"

"Not New York," he said with disgust. "Lakers by fifteen. Two minutes left in the third."

"Want me to fix us something for dinner?"

"Uh, no." He chuckled when she swatted him again. "You asked."

"We can order in."

"Fine with me. Oh, Savannah called. She said to give her a call."

She hadn't spoken to Savannah in days. She couldn't. With what she knew or at least suspected, she couldn't talk to Savannah without her friend knowing that something was wrong. But she couldn't avoid her forever. And she didn't want to. She missed her friend.

She pushed up from the couch. "I'll call now before it starts getting late. Decide what you want and order the same for me."

"Idiot!" he roared. "Where'd you learn how to play, from your grandma?"

Danielle shook her head and walked into the bedroom. She'd tell him about Mia's dinner party plans after the game. Anything she said now wouldn't even register.

Sitting down on the side of the bed, she stared at the phone. Finally she snatched it up and dialed Savannah's number.

"Okay, girl, don't cuss me out. I know it's been a minute," Danielle said the moment Savannah answered.

"I was wondering what was going on. Mia was gone, you disappear. How are you?"

"Great." She brought her up to date on what had been going on with the assignment, leaving out everything having to do with Bernard, and then told her about her meeting with Tasha.

"You have been busy. Is there any way I can help? You were in my corner when I had to deal with my first case."

"I think I'm okay. I'm running some checks on the people from the list." She lowered her voice. "Jasmine showed me how to have a search program run from the PDA while I'm doing other things. I set the search modes this morning. As soon as I can I'm going to check and see what came up."

"Great. But don't hesitate to ask if you need me."

"Oh, Mia is having a dinner party on Saturday to celebrate the engagement, but it's a surprise. So can you get your mom over there?"

"Sure, I'll tell her something. She's always happy to go to one of Mia's soirees."

"Something's wrong. I can hear it in your voice. What is it?"

Savannah blew out a breath through the phone. "You know how close me and my mother are?"

"Sure."

"Things have been really strained since she made her big announcement," she said with a hint of an edge to her voice.

Danielle totally understood Savannah's reservations. But hers were for entirely different reasons.

"As much as we don't want to accept it, Anna, Claudia is a grown woman, perfectly capable of making her own decisions."

"I know. It's just that it's so soon. She barely knows the man."

"Unfortunately, sis, it's not our decision to make. It's Claudia's."

"I know. I've had her to myself for so long, and with the baby coming, I want my mom," she said in an exaggerated whine.

Danielle laughed. "Girl, you need to stop. How are you feeling by the way?"

"Like I've gained ten pounds, which I did."

"How's Blake dealing with impending fatherhood and your extra pounds?"

"Blake is a dream. He says the nicest things even when my hormones are raging and I'm being a real bitch." She laughed. "And, girl...the sex is to die for. If I knew I could be this good, I would have made sure I got pregnant a long time ago!"

"You are a hot mess."

"Hot is the word. All the time. Anyway, it's good to hear your voice. I was beginning to feel like an orphan. No mother, no girlfriends...sniff, sniff."

Danielle cracked up. "You missed your calling on Broadway. I'll see you Saturday night."

"Looking forward to it."

Danielle hung up. Based on the roar coming from the living room, the game was still in full swing. She retrieved her PDA from her purse and powered it on.

Before she'd left for her meeting that morning, she'd set up a search protocol on Bernard. She'd plugged in all the information she had to date. She couldn't wait to see what the results were. She'd also submitted his image to the facial recognition databank, by using a picture they'd all taken several months earlier at Mia's gathering. It wasn't great but should be good enough.

Within moments the pages began to load. Danielle

scrolled and scrolled, her thoughts scrambling in disbelief and fear.

For all intents and purposes, Bernard Hassell didn't
exist. There was no record of him anywhere, at all.

How was that possible? There had to be something
wrong with the program.

But what if there wasn't?

Chapter 14

Danielle was in the shower, getting ready for the party and working out the plan in her head that she and Mia had discussed. It was risky. There was no question about it. But if she could pull it off, maybe she could finally get a lead.

The bathroom door opened and Nick came in. He slid open the shower door and stood there for a moment admiring Danielle before he got in and stood behind her.

"It's been all over the news," he crooned in her ear as he massaged her hips.

"What?" The word jerked out of her throat when his fingers slipped between her wet, slippery folds. She drew in a breath and shut her eyes.

"Water conservation. Everyone has to do their part."

She turned into his arms and faced him. "Is that what you heard?"

"Yep." He nibbled her neck, and she felt his erection press between her thighs.

She took his manhood in her palm and began massaging him in a slow up-and-down motion until he groaned with pleasure.

"We're going to be late," she whispered in his ear.

Steam enveloped them. The pulsing water cascaded around them.

"Looks that way."

He lifted her up and she wrapped her legs tightly around his waist—he pushed deep inside her.

Danielle put the finishing touches on her makeup while Nick finished getting dressed. "I promised Mia I would get there early to help." She spun toward him. "But someone distracted me," she added with a sly grin.

Nick chuckled. "Sorry," he singsonged, totally unapologetic. "Go on ahead and I'll meet you there."

"Thank, sweetie." She pecked him on the lips. "Don't be too long," she said, hurrying out.

"I won't."

As she opened the door to leave, she heard the distinct sound of the television turning on and the roar of a basketball game in progress. She shook her head and laughed.

"You two always look like you have a secret," Mia said when she came to the door and greeted Nick.

Danielle, who was standing in earshot, blushed as she

walked up to Nick, and images of what they'd done to each other in the shower flashed through her head.

"Come on in. Everyone is here," Danielle said, taking his hand.

Nick went straight to Savannah and wrapped her in a hug. "You look fabulous," he said, stepping back and taking a good look at her.

Savannah did a little curtsy. "Thank you."

"And how are you, proud papa to be?"

Blake grinned and beamed down at his wife. "Counting the days." He leaned forward and shook Nick's hand. "Long time, man. Good to see you."

"You, too. We have to stop waiting on Mia's dinner parties to hang out."

"For sure. As a matter of fact I have some tickets to the next Knicks game. She hates 'em," he added with a toss of his head in Savannah's direction.

"They're bound to be playing someone better than themselves, so why not?" Nick said with a chuckle.

The two men walked off to continue talking about sports.

Danielle asked about Claudia.

"She called a little while ago and said they were on their way."

A tingle of relief released the knot in her stomach. Everything hinged on Bernard's being there that night. Just then Steve Long, Mia's beau, came from the kitchen with a tray of finger food appetizers.

"Evenin' folks," he said. "This woman has had me chained to the stove all evening." He passed the tray around and greeted everyone amid bubbles of laughter.

Danielle had a minute to again question Mia. "Where are they?" she said in a whisper.

"On their way. Claudia said something had come up with Bernard at the last minute and they were running late."

"I don't want us to be in the middle of dinner when…"

The ringing doorbell cut her off in midsentence. Mia briefly clasped Danielle's wrist and squeezed lightly before heading for the door.

Squeals of laughter underscored by a gentle bass floated into the living room. Mia led the last of the guests inside.

"Sorry we're late," Claudia said, holding on to Bernard's hand.

"I hear congratulations are in order," Steve said, breaking out a bottle of champagne.

Mia followed him with a tray of champagne flutes and a bottle of sparkling cider for the mama-to-be.

"To Claudia and Bernard," Steve said, raising his glass.

"Claudia and Bernard!" the group chorused.

Glasses clinked all around.

Claudia looked up at Bernard with so much love in her eyes, and Danielle cringed because deep in her gut she knew that this man was not who he pretended to be.

Mia caught Danielle's eye while the guests were busy talking. Mia gave an almost imperceptible nod of her head.

"For those of you who don't know, this is a surprise engagement party," Danielle announced with a flourish.

"Oh, my goodness," Claudia said, covering her mouth with one hand and grabbing Bernard with her other. He swept her up in a hug.

Danielle slapped her palm against her forehead. "I need to run home. I forgot the gift."

"Oh, don't worry about it," Claudia said. "This is surprise enough," she said, beaming with delight.

"No, I wouldn't feel right, and I want you to have it on your special night. It won't take long. I'll be back before you know it."

Danielle rushed toward the door and darted out. She was in her car by the time Nick reached the top of the stairs. She pulled off without looking back.

Danielle checked the time on the dashboard. It was nine fifteen. It would take ten minutes to get there, do a quick five-minute search and ten minutes back. Her heart was racing like crazy.

Everything she needed was in her purse. She made a right turn at the next corner, got caught at a red light, then took a left. The house was on the next block. She checked the addresses on the right-hand side, slowed and parked two doors away.

Danielle grabbed her purse and took out the small makeup kit that held her burglary tools. She prayed that she would remember what Margaret had taught her and would not get herself arrested for breaking and entering.

Danielle looked both ways and jogged up the short flight of brick stairs to the front door. Her pulse was beating so hard and fast in her ears that she could barely hear the sounds around her.

Her hands shook as she took the pin and hook out of the case. She inserted them into the lock, pressing her free fingers against the door as she worked the tools. She felt the lock click open. A rush of air burst from her lungs. She stole a look behind her, then went inside.

She knew there had to be a computer there—somewhere. She needed to find it and get the information she needed.

A little more than five minutes later, she was locking the door behind her. She jogged down the stairs and hurried toward her car.

Then she stopped short.

"Nick."

Chapter 15

"Wh-what are you doing here?"

"I should be asking you that, Dani."

"You followed me?" she asked incredulously, trying to buy time.

"I tried to tell you that I would ride with you. Then I saw you go the wrong way to our house, so I followed you. Here."

Danielle looked everywhere but in Nick's accusing eyes. "I can't do this now." She made a move to get in her car. Nick grabbed her arm. Her gaze flew to where he held her.

"Don't walk away from me, Danielle. I want to know what's going on."

She looked right into his eyes. "Whatever you're thinking, you're wrong."

"You have no idea what I'm thinking!" he shouted, his voice echoing along the quiet street.

"You're right. I don't. But this isn't going to be solved on a street corner." She moved toward her car.

Nick hung his head. "Go ahead, leave." He turned and walked away.

"Nick! If you love me, you'll trust me."

He turned slowly toward her. "If you loved me, we wouldn't be here."

Something inside her seemed to break. She knew if she let him walk away he'd never come back, not this time. Everything was teetering on the edge, and a move in any direction would send it all crashing to the ground.

Nick opened the door to his car.

"I promise to explain everything. Please, you have to trust me." Her voice cracked with emotion. "Please."

Nick hesitated with his hand on the handle of the car door. "Make my excuses to your friends." He got in the car, and with Danielle watching he drove off.

Danielle didn't know what to expect when she came home from the party several hours later.

When she'd returned to the party with Claudia's gift which she'd stashed in the trunk earlier, she'd told the guests that Nick wasn't feeling well and had gone home. Only Mia guessed what really had transpired. Danielle hadn't explained much while they cleaned up the kitchen. Mia had tried to assure her that everything would work out.

But as she headed home that night and walked toward her bedroom, she wasn't too sure. She stepped inside— Nick was sitting in the dark on the edge of the bed.

"Nick, I—"

"Don't. I need you to listen, okay?" He spoke so quietly that she wasn't sure she'd heard him.

She stepped farther into the room but dared not get too close. Her heart thumped as she braced herself for the worst.

"When I met you, I thought…finally, the woman I'd been born to love. All the ugliness that was my life was wiped away when you smiled. The emptiness that I'd lived with since my dad died was filled with your presence. I wasn't lonely anymore. I felt that I'd found myself. I wasn't adrift. That was because of you." He turned toward her. "But now I don't know who I fell in love with. Maybe it was only my imagination. I wanted it so bad that I made you real. And if I don't know who you are, then maybe I don't know myself either."

Tears stung her eyes. She searched for the words to make it all okay, but she couldn't find them.

Nick pushed up from the bed and came toward her. "All I ever wanted was someone who was going to be as real with me as I was with them. I thought that's what we had. I was wrong."

"Please don't go," she whispered. "All I can say is that…I'm working on something and right now I can't tell you about it."

He looked at her and shook his head. "Goodbye, Danielle." He walked toward the door, and that was when she noticed the suitcase.

She heard herself calling his name, knew that her feet were moving, running behind him. But like waking from a dream she realized that she was in the room alone and Nick was gone.

* * *

By morning Danielle's eyes were so red and swollen from crying all night that she could barely see. Worn out, frustrated and totally miserable, she stumbled into the kitchen to put on a pot of coffee. She had to pull herself together. There was a shoot scheduled for the afternoon, and she knew that Nick would be there. No way would she allow him to see the mess that she'd become in only a matter of hours.

As the coffee brewed, the events of the previous night ran through her head like a bad movie. The only saving grace was the information she'd gained on Bernard.

After breaking into his apartment, she'd located his computer in a small room in the back of the one-bedroom duplex.

She'd used a USB hookup to download his files onto a memory stick. While the information was being transferred, she had done a quick search of his bedroom. What she'd discovered still had her mind reeling, and she wasn't sure what to make of it—passports and driver's licenses with four different aliases. So who was Bernard Hassell?

With her coffee cup in hand, she returned to her bedroom and retrieved the memory stick from her purse. She plugged it into her laptop and massaged her temples with the tips of her fingers while she waited. Her head pounded from lack of sleep, and she'd cried so much that she was totally dehydrated.

But at least for a little while she could focus on someone else's issues instead of her own, for which she had no easy answers. She rubbed her eyes, took a long swallow of coffee and watched the information appear on the screen.

The more she read, the more disturbed she became. The ringing telephone drew her attention away from the damning information.

She reached across the bed, hesitating for a moment. What if it was Nick? What would she say? Would she have sense enough to find her voice this time and tell him what was in her heart?

Her shaky hand hovered over the receiver. It rang for the fourth time. If she waited for the next ring, it would be sent to their voice-mail service.

Danielle drew in a breath and snatched up the phone. "Hello?" Her heart pounded.

"Dani, it's Mia. I was calling to see if you were all right. I know that story you gave us about Nick last night was B.S. What happened? He darted out of here. You come back alone, looking like you'd been struck by lightning…"

Danielle leaned back against the thick down pillows, drew in a long breath and spilled the story about what she'd found in Bernard's apartment—including Nick's appearance in front of Bernard's house.

"Oh, dayum," Mia murmured. "What are you going to do?"

"I've been asking myself that question since I found out. But my own life is so screwed up that I can't even think straight."

They both sighed, deep in thought.

"I think it's time you told Savannah," Mia said.

"I've been thinking the same thing. Can you meet me at The Shop at noon?"

"I'll be there. And I'll give Savannah a call and tell her it's important and that she needs to take an early lunch."

"Thanks. See you in a few."

By the time Savannah arrived, a bit breathless, Danielle and Mia were already seated in their favorite booth.

"What's the big emergency?" she asked while taking her seat. She looked from one gloomy face to the other. "Somebody better tell me something. You're making me nervous."

Mia looked to Danielle and gave a short nod of her head.

Danielle pressed her lips together in concentration and looked directly at Savannah. "It's a long story. But it's all related to the assignment and Bernard…."

"Oh…my…God," Savannah said between the fingers that covered her mouth when Danielle brought her story to a close. "I… My mother." Tears filled her eyes but they didn't fall. "I knew it. I knew something was wrong." She frowned, her dark eyes were like laser beams as they zeroed in on Danielle. "I'm going over there." She started up from her seat, and Mia grabbed her wrist.

"No, you're not! That's not an option." She turned to Danielle. "*You* need to confront him."

"What! Are you crazy? I don't want to wind up a statistic in the news—or worse, never make the head-lines because I've simply vanished," she said, her voice rising in alarm.

"Look, you've verified the fact that he was in the service, but not as Bernard Hassell. Use that as leverage."

"I don't see how."

"Tell him that you will spill it all to Claudia," Savannah offered.

"What if he doesn't care and sees me as a threat to whatever it is he's up to?"

"What if he *does* care?" Mia said, always the romantic.

Danielle sighed heavily. "I don't know…"

"Do it somewhere safe," Savannah said.

"Like where?"

"Your place," Mia said.

"You have got to be kidding."

"No, seriously. You said that he and Nick were friends, right. Well, tell him you need to talk to him about Nick. Tell him Nick left and you're worried about him. And you need his advice."

Danielle thought about it. "Maybe it could work," she said slowly, not completely convinced.

"I'll be there as well—out of sight."

"Me, too," Savannah said.

"No, you won't!" the duo responded.

Savannah puffed and pouted, folding her arms over her growing baby bump.

"Okay," Danielle conceded. "If we can get to Bernard, or whoever he is, I know it's going to lead us to the people behind the identity theft operation."

"By the way," Mia said, "I've checked with everyone I know and everyone they know, and not a soul has ever heard of Bernard Hassell."

Chapter 16

Nick awoke with every bone in his body aching. His eyes squinted open and he turned, barely catching himself before falling off the couch.

He expelled an expletive as he hoisted himself back up and took a look around, trying to get his bearings. Nothing looked familiar. He pushed himself into a sitting position and the inside of his brain did a rapid 360-degree turn. His stomach lurched to his throat, and he was a gulp away from spewing its contents all over this rug that he didn't recognize.

"You're up."

Nick's hazy gaze moved in the direction of the voice. He squinted the image into focus. "Bernard?" he asked in confusion.

Bernard grinned and slowly approached. He handed

him a glass of tomato juice and two aspirin. "Take these. You'll feel better—eventually."

Nick tossed down the aspirin, then ran his fingers through his spiky hair. "How did I get here, and what was I doing before I arrived?" His tongue felt like an old slipper.

"After you left the party, you never returned. I guess you must have spent the next few hours drinking at Bob & Lou's Bar and Lounge up on Amsterdam Avenue. The owner called me about three this morning. He said you told him to call. He found my name in your cell phone. I picked you up—literally—and brought you here. You kept insisting that you weren't going home."

Bernard took a seat opposite Nick. He leaned forward, bracing his arms on his thighs. "You want to tell me why you didn't want to go home?"

"It's complicated." He rubbed his brow. "Me and Dani…she's keeping things from me, lying, doing stuff that she can't explain, but she wants me to trust her. She begged me to trust her. But I can't, not anymore, not if she can't be honest with me."

Bernard was thoughtful for a moment, knowing that what he said next could affect Nick's relationship with Danielle for good.

"Sometimes, man, you gotta let go of all the things that ground you and step out on faith."

Nick glared at him.

"Do you believe in God?"

The question threw him. "Yeah, why?"

"You believe that there is a God even though you can't see God or hear God, right? You believe not because of anything concrete but because of what you feel in your mind and in your heart."

Nick's jaw clenched.

"Same thing with love, man. You can't see it or touch it, but you believe in it. You know it's real because you can feel it in your heart and in your head even if you can't explain it."

"What's that got to do with what Dani did?"

"Sometimes you just have to believe, son, simple as that. Give her a chance."

He stood. "I put some fresh towels in the bathroom. There's plenty of food in the fridge. Make yourself at home. I need to run out for about an hour."

Nick's thoughts were still plowing through what Bernard had said when a thought struck him. "My car? I think I drove." He looked up at Bernard. "Did I?"

Bernard grinned. "I'm going to pick up your car now. The bartender wisely kept your keys and gave them to me when I got there." He lifted them from his pocket and shook them in the air. "See you in a few."

"Thanks, man."

"Don't worry about it." He walked toward the door. "At least think about what I said. Sometimes, things aren't as apparent as they appear." He opened the door and walked out.

Nick slowly got up from the couch and walked to the window. He watched Bernard drive off, and the events of the previous night began to come clear. He could see himself standing in front of the building, imagining the worst when he saw Danielle go inside. He could still hear her plead with him to "trust her."

His jaw clenched. He'd told Bernard everything except that where he'd followed Danielle wasn't to some random house, but *his*. He wondered what sage advice Bernard would offer if he had known that bit of information.

Chapter 17

Danielle went through the motions at the photo shoot, setting the scenes, coaxing the models and motivating her crew. Thank goodness for Mark. He was an excellent photographer and filled in on a moment's notice for Nick.

She'd expected Nick to be there. She'd expected that even if he pretended she didn't exist, she could at least see him and maybe he could tell by looking into her eyes how much she cared and how sorry she was for messing things up between them.

All through the night, through the tears, fits of anger and frustration, she silently prayed that if Nick just gave her one more chance, she would tell him she loved him. She would say the words from the bottom of her heart.

But as the hours ticked by, it became apparent that he wasn't coming and she grew more and more on edge.

He'd never done that before. He'd never missed a session and surely never missed one and didn't call.

She flipped open her cell-phone case that hung on her hip. At least if she could hear his voice, she would know that he was okay.

Nick stepped out of the shower, running a towel over his wet hair. He was beginning to feel halfway human again. He was staring in the mirror, accessing his red-rimmed eyes, when the ringing of his cell phone pulled him in the direction of the living room, where he'd left his pile of clothes. He dug through his shirt and dress slacks and found it beneath his socks.

He flipped the front cover open. The familiar number registered on the screen. He stared at it, listened until the ringing stopped and then tossed the phone onto the couch.

The tightness in Danielle's throat was almost un-bearable. She listened to Nick's recorded voice, the one that soothed her, teased her, whispered in her ear. She didn't bother to leave a message. She returned back to the set and tried to concentrate but couldn't. Her thoughts kept shifting back to Nick. Maybe he was hurt, lying in a ditch somewhere. Maybe he was sick and needed someone to look after him. He could have been in an accident.

The ugly scenarios kept repeating and repeating in her head on a continuous loop until she thought she'd scream—and she did.

"Break! Twenty minutes." Her breathing escalated with the anxiety that was making her crazy.

Gladys, one of her crew members, who handled the lights, asked her if she was sick, because she didn't look well, and Danielle nearly burst into tears. She knew she was on the verge of breaking, and that reality shook her up even more.

The fact that she had allowed her feelings for someone else to get the best of her, cloud her thoughts and confuse her judgment was way more than she was prepared to deal with.

Danielle Holloway was used to being in charge. She called the shots both in relationships and out. This whole thing with Nick was new and it was scary.

And to complicate matters further, she had the Cartel assignment to fulfill, and the more she found out, the worse things became.

She glanced up and saw Reggie, one of her cameramen, walking past her.

"Hey, Reggie."

He stopped and turned. Danielle approached him. "Listen, I need to take care of some things. Do you think you can handle the rest of the shoot for today? We have nineteen more cityscape shots and two indoors. Mark will guide you through what needs to be done."

"Sure," he said, seemingly thrilled by the chance.

"Just follow the shot sheet. Melody will keep the models in order."

"Not a problem, Dani. Thanks for the chance."

She nodded and hurried off toward her car before she could change her mind.

The "brain trust"—her, Mia and Savannah—had come up with the brilliant idea of having her confront

Bernard using the ruse that she needed his advice on how to handle the mess between her and Nick.

But what she needed now was to know that he was all right. And the only person she could think of who could tell her was Bernard, or whatever his name was.

If something had happened to Nick because of her, she'd never forgive herself. She got behind the wheel of her vehicle, took her PDA out of her bag and pulled up everything she had on Bernard Hassell. Jasmine had finally been able to work her magic and come up with landline and cell-phone numbers for Bernard. Danielle wasn't sure how she'd missed it when she'd done her own search, but Jasmine was, after all, a true techie.

Danielle tried the cell first.

Bernard picked up on the second ring. "Hello, Danielle. I wondered how long it was going to take you to get to me."

Frowning, she jerked back from the voice on the phone. "What?"

"Meet me at the corner of West Fourth and Houston in twenty minutes." He disconnected the call.

Shit. Had Nick told him that she'd broken into his house? No. It didn't sound as if he was upset, more as if he was *expecting* her call. He *was* expecting her call. He'd said as much.

She shook her head in confusion and caught a glimpse of the dashboard clock. It was already after three. It would take her the full twenty minutes and then some to get to the Village from midtown at that time of day.

Danielle put the car in gear and eased into traffic. What if this was some kind of setup? If he'd been expecting her call, then he may know more about her than she realized.

One of the first things explained in the CD lessons was to always be aware of potential traps and going into situations when no one else knew where you were.

It wasn't likely he would try anything in broad daylight on a busy street corner, but the cold truth was that people disappeared off New York City streets every day. She didn't intend to be one of them.

Danielle got her cell and speed-dialed Mia's number. She quickly ran down the troubling conversation and told her where she was going—*just in case.*

"This doesn't sound good, Dani. Don't do anything stupid. I can meet you."

"No. Just stay available. If you don't hear from me in an hour, call Savannah. She'll know what to do. Gotta go."

The trip felt as if it were taking forever. She must have hit every red light in lower Manhattan. By the time she arrived, her nerves were so frazzled that she was damp all over. She found a spot at a meter and parked.

Danielle looked around. The streets were full of activity. That was a good thing. The more people there were, the better she felt. She got out of the SUV, fed the meter and began walking toward the meeting place a block away and spotted Bernard leaning against a mailbox. He was casually dressed in a pair of khaki pants, brown loafers and a tan windbreaker.

She took a good look around before going any farther. Her trained photographic eye scouted out the stores, the entrance to the train station and the shortest distance back to her car. Drawing in a deep breath, she walked forward.

Bernard seemed to sense her and turned in her direction. It struck her again how much he resembled Billy Dee Williams. He could probably get plenty of work with that woman she'd met on the elevator.

Danielle lifted her chin, putting on a façade of bravado that eluded her.

Bernard actually smiled at her. "Glad you could make it. Let's walk and talk." He started off without waiting for her response. She picked up her pace. Her ponytail bounced with every step, and she was glad that she'd kept on her sneakers in case she needed to make a run for it. She caught up with him.

He made a right onto a short residential block away from the heavy flow of traffic on West Fourth Street. Her throat grew dry.

"Where are we going?"

"I'm sure you must be concerned about Nick," he said rather than answer her question.

Her breath stuck in her chest. Was Nick a hostage? "Yes."

"He's fine. A little hungover but fine. He's at my place. You know where that is, don't you?"

She curled her hands into fists to keep them from shaking.

He pressed his hand against the small of her back and steered her around the corner. The sounds of vehicular and pedestrian noises grew faint. Her feet suddenly felt like lead.

"I know all about what you're doing," he said, stopping in front of an abandoned building.

Her eyes widened in alarm. She began to back away.

Bernard reached inside his jacket, and Danielle bolted for the corner, which seemed to get farther away with every step she took. Her car was now more than three blocks away. She hadn't run farther than to the bathroom in ages, she thought frantically. He, on the other hand, was in shape. He'd catch her before she made it to the corner. She could almost feel the heat of a bullet tearing through her back.

A heavy hand grabbed her shoulder, nearly spinning her around. She screamed.

"Cell phone, cell phone," he said, pushing it in front of her face. "Here, Jean wants to speak to you."

She was breathing so hard she was dizzy. It took several moments before what he said registered. She stared at him in disbelief. Nothing made sense.

He pushed the phone toward her. "Take it, Danielle. Jean will explain everything."

Slowly she reached for the phone and brought it to her ear without taking her eyes off Bernard. "Hello…"

Danielle listened in stunned silence as Jean explained that Bernard was working with her from the Office of Homeland Security and that information had been planted in her files about Bernard to test Danielle to see how strong her instincts were.

"Th-this was all part of a test!" She didn't know whether to laugh or cry. And she'd passed with flying colors, according to Jean, who was proud to officially declare Danielle a member of The Ladies Cartel. In addition to which Bernard would be her contact and her partner.

Danielle slumped back against a streetlamp and gazed

at Bernard. She was waiting for Ashton Kutcher to jump out of a van and tell her that she'd been "punk'd."

"Sorry I had to be so mysterious, but we needed to know you had what it took to do the job."

Danielle drew in a long breath. "You've been watching me all along—and Nick?"

He nodded.

"You befriended him. He likes you. Is that all part of the plan?" She felt her anger begin to rise. It was one thing to screw around with her—she'd invited it by getting involved with the Cartel—but screwing around with Nick was a different story.

"It was in the beginning, but I like Nick. I really like him and he loves you…deeply." He looked right in her eyes. "And I think right about now he'd be willing to listen to you."

"Does Claudia know?" she asked as they walked back to the car.

Bernard turned to her and grinned. "Of course. It was her idea."

Danielle shook her head. This was all too much to process, but when she got it together, she was going to spill it all to the girls.

They reached where Bernard was parked, and she realized he was driving Nick's car.

"Long story," he said when he saw the question form on her lips. "Hop in. I'll take you to your car and explain on the way."

Chapter 18

Bernard opened the door to his small house and stepped aside to let Danielle pass.

Nick glanced up, then did a double take when he saw Danielle standing there looking a little lost and uncertain.

He got up from the couch but didn't come toward her.

Bernard cleared his throat. "Uh, I forgot…ice cream." He backed out of the door and left them alone.

Danielle clasped her hands in front of her.

Silence dragged out between them, then they both spoke at once.

"You first," Nick conceded, with a nervous laugh.

Danielle took a tentative step toward him.

"I'm so sorry, Nick. I should have told you in the beginning what was going on," she began. "Claudia is planning a surprise party for Bernard, and she needed to get a list of his friends without him knowing. We figured that during the party would be a perfect time, and I volunteered." She nearly choked on the lie she and Bernard had concocted in the car with Claudia's help.

Nick squeezed his eyes shut and shook his head. He threw his hands up in the air. "What? Why didn't you just tell me?"

"Because you can't keep a secret," she said with a sly grin.

"I can't keep a secret?" he asked, sounding mildly offended.

Danielle planted her right hand on her hip and cocked her head to the side, her ponytail swinging in the process. "No. Weren't you the one who blabbed to Reggie that Gladys liked him, and didn't you tell Savannah about the present that Blake was getting her when they found out she was pregnant. And the time—"

He held his palms up. "All right, all right, I give up. But—" he shook a finger at her "—I didn't tell the crew about us." He came to stand in front of her, his brows knitted tightly. He looked down into her eyes. "I should have listened to you," he said softly. "I let fear and ego mess with my head instead of listening to my heart and trusting you and my feelings."

Danielle felt a sick sensation sweep through her stomach as she listened to him confess to his faults, which were built on her lies. It took all she had not to break down and confess the whole twisted story. But she knew she couldn't, especially now that she had been truly validated as a member, one who was willing to risk everything to be one.

Danielle put a finger to his lips and slowly shook her head. "There was no way for you to know. It was just a colossal case of miscommunication."

He angled his head to the side and slid his arms around her waist, pulling her close. "What can I do to make it up to you?" he asked, bending down to plant a trail of featherlight kisses along her neck.

Danielle sighed breathlessly. Her eyes fluttered closed for a moment as she relished in his touch. "Why don't we take up this conversation in the privacy of our home," she whispered.

"There you go reading my mind…"

The instant the door shut behind them, Danielle and Nick were pulling off clothes, kicking off shoes, grabbing, kissing, stumbling and laughing all the way to the bedroom, where they collapsed onto the bed in a tangle of legs, arms and exploring tongues and hands.

Their hearty laughter slowly ebbed into low moans and deep sighs as the fever that heated their bodies rose by degrees and the playfulness shifted to heighten their sensual pleasures.

Danielle toyed with Nick, teasing him with tiny nibbles and long laps of her tongue along his warm flesh. Her fingers traced the hard outline of his chest, drifting down to his hard stomach to nestle for a moment in the downy soft hair that surrounded his pulsing erection.

"I have some making up to do myself," she whispered, looking up at him for an instant before she drew his length into her mouth.

A groan from deep in his throat rose up and punctuated the air. He gripped the sheets in his fist and forced himself not to fully bury his need in her throat.

Danielle worked him with long licks of her tongue, sucking him in and out, feeling his erection pulse in her mouth until he was a stroke away from exploding. The sensations grew so intense that he begged her to stop, holding her head in the palms of his hands to keep her from making him lose the last bit of control he had.

"I want you, Dani," he groaned. "I need to be inside you."

Slowly she crept up the length of his body, planting tiny kisses along his heated flesh until she was astride him. She taunted the tip of him with slow rotations of her hips allowing him to only barely touch her wet folds.

Then suddenly, Nick turned her onto her back, pinning her beneath him with his weight. He pushed her thighs wide apart with his knees and found his way home.

They made love off and on through the night, sometimes slow and easy and at others with a hunger that couldn't seem to be filled except with more of the same.

The light from the full moon slid in between the curtains, casting a soft glow in the room. A faint breeze gently lifted the curtains from the window.

Dani lay curled against Nick, her arm draped loosely across his chest. Tenderly he stroked her curves and realized how badly he could have screwed up simply because he couldn't let go of a past that denied him happiness. He wouldn't listen when she tried to explain. There was a part of him that believed that because of what happened with his father, he didn't deserve to be happy and if he was happy, it would be taken from him.

To avoid that, he wanted to strike first, and it had nearly cost him the woman he loved.

He held her a bit tighter, listening to the soft cadence of her breathing. Losing Danielle was something he would never risk again. In order to ensure that, he would have to be honest with her and let go of the ghost that haunted him.

"Babe," he said softly. "I want to talk to you about something."

Danielle snuggled deeper into the pillow and muttered something unintelligible.

Nick smiled ruefully, kissed the top of her head and closed his eyes. Tomorrow was another day, he thought as he drifted into a deep, satisfied sleep.

When Danielle awoke the next morning, the space next to her was empty. Slowly she sat up, rubbed her eyes and sniffed the air. Hmm, bacon. Nick was busy in the kitchen doing his thing.

While he was busy, she decided to quickly check her PDA. Now that she and Bernard were on the same side, she could scratch him off her most-wanted list and direct her attention elsewhere.

She retrieved the PDA from her purse and immediately noticed the blinking light, indicating a message was waiting. It was from Bernard. He needed to talk to her right way.

With her eye on the door, she quickly dialed Bernard's number on her cell phone.

"I have some information, a lead," he said without preamble. "There's a couple—Jenna and Anthony

Taylor—that have been on our radar for a while, but we can't prove anything. They're a little too low on my totem pole, but I have a gut feeling that they may be at the heart of your assignment. They live in a co-op on East 72nd Street. You need to get close to them."

"How?"

"You'll figure it out."

He disconnected the call.

Danielle sat on the side of the bed with the phone still in her hand. *Jenna and Anthony Taylor.* The names sounded so familiar, but she couldn't place them.

She didn't have a shoot today, which was a good thing, but the flip side of that was neither did Nick. Generally on their days off they spent time together just hanging out, going to the movies, going shopping, visiting a new restaurant or, their favorite pastime, checking out new photography equipment. She knew that as soon as they finished breakfast, he was going to ask her what she wanted to do today.

As her thoughts went through a variety of scenarios she could tell him, the phone rang.

"Hello?"

"Just how long do you plan to make me wait before you tell me what the hell is going on with Bernard?" Savannah snapped into the phone.

Danielle tossed her head back and scrunched up her face. She'd gotten so caught up in the events of the day and night before that she'd totally forgotten to let Savannah know her mother wasn't in love with Jack the Ripper after all.

"Anna, I am so sorry, girl. Yesterday was crazy, to say the least. But I know I should have called you. First and foremost, everything is fine and that includes Bernard." She went on to explain all that had happened, up to and including her most recent conversation with Bernard.

"I still can hardly believe it," Savannah said. "Bernard is with Homeland Security, and it was my mother's idea all along. I'll be damned."

"Yeah, who you telling? I felt the same way. I guess that's why your mom is so good at what she does for the Cartel."

"I guess so," Savannah said in awe. "Now what are you going to do about the couple?"

"That's what I was trying to work out when you called. But I swear their names sound so familiar."

"Who did you say they were again?"

"Jenna and Anthony Taylor."

"Hmm, I wonder if they are the same couple that were clients of Mia's about a year or so ago. Remember some hotshot couple that had this fabulous party on a yacht?"

"Yeah, right," she said slowly as the recollection began to take shape. "I wonder if they are the same people."

"One way to find out."

They got Mia on the line with three-way calling.

"Sure sounds like them," Mia said. "Let me check my database to confirm the address. Hang on a sec."

Several moments later Mia returned to the phone. "It's them. I can't believe I was dealing with con artists," Mia said, more annoyed than alarmed. Her reputation was built on dealing with the crème of the crop. If word of this got out, her business would suffer.

"What are you going to do?" Mia inquired.

"I'm going over there for starters. But first I've got to keep Nick occupied."

"How?"

"I'll let his new best buddy, Bernard, handle it."

Chapter 19

Danielle cruised to a stop on the opposite side of the street from 425 East 72nd Street. It was a twenty-story high-rise with rent hovering in the million-dollar category. She took out her camera from her knapsack and adjusted the telephoto lens, hoping she would remember the couple when and if she saw them. But just in case, she planned to take a picture of everyone who came in and out and then run the photos past Mia.

The doorman opened the door for an older couple to exit. Although Danielle was pretty sure they weren't who she was looking for, she snapped them anyway.

This process went on for about a half hour, when a police cruiser slowed and stopped next to her car. At first she thought they'd stopped for a red light—until both officers got out of the cruiser. One approached her window; the other went to the passenger side.

Oh, Lawd. "Yes, Officer?" she said sweetly. Meanwhile cop number two was peering inside her vehicle.

"License and registration."

She swallowed hard. In her entire life she'd never been stopped by the police. She'd heard and read the stories of the "mishaps" of innocent drivers being pulled over by police for what they claimed were routine traffic stops. Oh, Lawd. She reached for her purse, took out her wallet and found her license and registration. She handed both to him with a soft smile.

"Step out of the van, please, miss."

Were they going to arrest her? Would she wind up a cause celebre for the good Reverend Al Sharpton? Or a statistic?

She slowly opened the car door and stepped out.

"We got a report that someone was sitting out here taking pictures," the officer said.

"Is this your equipment, ma'am?" the second officer asked.

She looked over her shoulder as he extracted her camera bag and camera from the passenger seat. "Yes."

The first cop was still looking at her paperwork as if he were committing it to memory. Finally he handed it back.

"What are you doing here?"

"I'm a fashion photographer. I was simply scouting out locations for possible photo shoots…Officer."

"You have any proof of that?"

Her mind scrambled, trying to visualize the contents of her wallet. Then she remembered she still had the

Michael Preston contract in her purse, which she was supposed to have filed away but for some reason never did. She leaned inside the car, dug around in her over-size purse and pulled out the folded manila envelope. She took out the contract and handed it to him.

"Michael Preston. The designer from that runway show?" he asked, mildly impressed.

"Yes." She beamed him a smile.

"My wife watches that show all the time." He looked at her with a new kind of respect. "What's he like?"

She was about to answer when she saw movement coming from across the street. She wanted to push the cop out of the way to be sure she was seeing correctly. It was that woman from the elevator—the one with the modeling agency.

"Ma'am?"

"Oh, I wish I knew. Every time I've gone to his office, I've dealt with his assistant." The woman got into a waiting cab, and it sped away.

"Yeah, I guess he can afford one, right?" He chuckled as if he'd just shared a joke with his best friend. He handed her back the contract. "All right. You can go but I suggest you find another spot. Apparently the neighbors in this area don't take kindly to being photographed."

"Thanks, Officer," she said and wondered if he heard her heavy sigh of relief.

"Have a nice day. And good luck."

"Thanks."

The officers returned to their car and pulled off. Her entire body was trembling so badly she barely made it back inside her vehicle. She lowered her head to the steering wheel and drew in several deep breaths. She'd have to find another way, she thought, as she put the car in gear. What was that woman doing there? Was she a tenant? Was she visiting someone? And how much of a coincidence was it that she handled look-alikes and the people Danielle was investigating dealt in stealing identities?

She had the woman's card, somewhere. Maybe it was time to give her a call and use her Alicia Keys looks to her advantage. She put the car in gear and pulled off.

When she returned home, she was surprised to find Nick sitting in front of the television.

"Hey, I thought you and Bernard were hanging out for the afternoon." She put her bag on the table in the hallway and walked toward him. But the closer she came, the expression on his face grew clearer and she saw what he held in his hand. Her heart thumped with dread.

He flipped the small compact around his hand.

She came to stand in front of him, and that was when she also noticed her TLC kit sitting at his feet.

"I got back early," he said. "I wanted to surprise you with a romantic dinner." He turned the compact around in his hand again. "I found this on the floor in the bedroom. Thought I was helping when I went to look for this—" he nodded toward her case at his feet "—to put it back." He looked up at her stricken face. "You want to tell me what all this is, Dani, 'cause it sure as hell ain't makeup!"

The few seconds that ticked by felt like an eternity as Danielle tried to figure out how she could possibly explain what he'd found. Her brain grinded to a halt.

"Don't you have anything to say?"

Her shoulders slumped. She could spend the next hour weaving one lie after another that she could never take back and have to continue building their relationship on lies.

Slowly she sat down next to him. She was about to break every rule she'd sworn to uphold. It may ruin her future with the Cartel, but she wasn't going to ruin her relationship with Nick.

Danielle turned to him. "I know what I'm about to tell you is going to sound crazy. And I'm breaking a major trust to say anything." She drew in a breath as she put her thoughts in order. "If I'm going to trust you with what I'm about to say, then you need to trust me as well and not ask me any questions. Just listen."

"What?" he asked in disbelief. "I'm a technician, Danielle. I know electronic equipment when I see it. You can no more tell me this is a compact than you can say there's no racism in America! And you're going to sit there and tell me that I simply have to *trust* you and not ask any questions!" He jumped up from the couch and spun toward her. "What…the next thing you're gonna tell me is that you're some kind of spy or something?"

"Something like that," she said, noticing his stunned expression, which quickly turned to outraged laughter. "Danielle, please don't insult my intelligence." He began to pace. "Listening devices, burglary tools! Who are you?"

"Nick, please listen to me. That's all I ask. And when I'm done, if you still don't believe me…then I'll accept whatever decision you make. But at least give me a chance." She paused. "Please."

His jaw flexed over and over, making the veins in his

temples pump. Finally he sat down and braced his arms on his thighs. "I'm listening."

More than an hour later, Danielle sat drained but surprisingly relieved as she waited for Nick's verdict.

He slowly shook his head. It was almost too crazy to comprehend. But the brilliance of it didn't escape him. Who would ever suspect the everyday woman to be a quasi-undercover agent? It's like the suburban housewives who run lucrative escort services during the week and take their kids to soccer practice on the weekend.

Nick turned to look at her, searching for any deception in her eyes but finding none.

She'd told him all she could reasonably tell him, leaving out the location of the Cartel, as well as the fact that not only was Savannah a card-carrying member, but also she was recruited by her mother, Claudia, who was one of the highest-ranking members in the organization.

Nick mopped his face with his hands. "How long have you been involved?" he asked.

"This is my first assignment, and I'll probably get kicked out because of this." She took his hands. "You have to swear to me that you will never, ever say anything to anyone. Please. It's one thing for me to mess up, but I can't ruin it for everyone else."

He nodded, then looked directly into her eyes. "You can trust me," he said with quiet sincerity. He opened the case at his feet. "I pretty much figured out what most of the gadgets were," he said, "but—" he lifted a bottle of what looked like shower gel and held it up "—what is this?"

She half grinned. "It's a sedative."

"Wow." He lifted the top tray, beneath which was an outline in the shape of a gun. "Please tell me that you're not carrying a gun around."

"No. I didn't get that far in my training. This was kind of a rush assignment."

"Is that where you've been this morning, on assignment?"

She nodded.

"Dani, I… This is all so crazy. I mean…" He turned to her, trying to find the words. "If you wind up with some kind of assignment that has you carrying a gun, I'd be insane with worry." He raked his fingers through his short ink-black hair. "And every time you walk out of the door and I don't know where you are…" His voice drifted off, but the implication hung in the air between them.

She studied the lines of anxiety that knitted his forehead. And then an idea slowly began to form. "We're a team right?"

"Yeah, absolutely."

"And we trust each other, right?"

"Yes, but that isn't going to stop me from worrying about you."

"But what if…you helped me."

His head jerked back in surprise. "Help you? But you said—"

"I know what I said," she interjected, cutting him off. "But I've already screwed up. This will probably be my first and last assignment anyway, so I might as well go out with a bang." A slow smile crept across her mouth.

"Let me explain to you what I have to do, and when I'm done, if you want to help me…then we go for it."

He tugged on his bottom lip with his teeth, a habit he had whenever he was contemplating his next move. "Shoot," he said, quickly adding, "and I meant that figuratively."

Chapter 20

The following day Danielle made an appointment to meet with Reba McDonald, the woman she'd met on the elevator, then saw coming from the building that she'd been staking out. Reba was more than happy to make time in her schedule to "squeeze" Danielle in.

All she needed was a few minutes of alone time in Reba's office to plant a transmitter on her phone and, if she had time, a tracking device on her computer. After pulling into the parking garage, she walked the short block to the office building.

She checked the minicamera that was attached to the clasp on her purse and called Nick on her cell phone.

"Is the picture coming through?" she asked.

"Clear as crystal," he said from his spot in front of the laptop in their home office. "Babe…"

"Yes?"

"Don't do anything silly, okay?"

"I won't. And you either. If things get strange, don't play hero and call the police. They can't be involved. Understood?"

"Yeah, yeah. Hey, good luck, 007."

"Very funny," she said with a light laugh. "See you on the other side."

Danielle pushed open the glass doors and rode the elevator up to the twentieth floor. She checked the directional sign for room 2018. She made a left turn down the corridor, and it was the last suite on the right.

She knocked on the door and through an intercom was asked whom she was there to see. She gave them Reba's name and was buzzed in.

"Hi," she said, forcing more cheer than necessary into her voice and then realizing how nervous she really was. "I'm Danielle Holloway."

The young woman looked Danielle over and then smiled. "Yep, Reba said you looked like Alicia's twin. Have a seat," she said, lifting her dimpled chin in the direction of a white leather love seat embraced on either side by two glass tables, which were decorated with the latest celebrity magazines.

Danielle settled herself and took a cursory look around. The walls were adorned with photographs of celebrities, covering everyone from rap artists to Oscar winners and everyone in between.

"They look like the real thing, don't they?"

Danielle turned in the direction of the voice. Reba approached. She stood no more than five foot five in heels.

Her gunmetal gray hair was cut to frame her rather angular face with the purpose of softening her square chin. She wore a fitted navy-blue suit that showed off her remarkable legs and narrow waist.

Danielle got up. "Are you saying that all of those photos are look-alikes?"

Reba nodded. "That's what I do. Sometimes a celeb needs a stand-in to get the press off them, and they come to me. Other times, it's for other reasons." She flashed a tight smile. "Come into my office and let's talk about what I can do for you."

Said the spider to the fly, Danielle thought as she followed Reba to her office.

"Make yourself comfortable." She indicated a chair placed beneath a circular table in the small but well-put-together office. Reba's desk was the focal point; it measured at least six feet long with a glass overlay beneath which looked like a massive collage of photographs. Danielle was most interested in the computer, which sat on the end of the desk.

Behind the desk, the twelve-foot windows displayed the might of towering Manhattan. There were several photos on the wall of Reba posing with some recognizable politicians, and the young actress from *Dreamgirls*.

"Are those real?" Danielle asked.

Reba chuckled. "What do you think?"

"I'm not really sure."

"Good, then I've done my job. Now, let me tell you what I think we can do. I cover everything from decoys to surprise guests for birthday parties. I think you would be great for parties."

"Really?" She hesitated, intentionally trying to give the impression that she may be broaching a sensitive topic. She leaned forward slightly. "Uh, you mentioned when we first met that these jobs pay very well."

"Absolutely."

"Well, I'm in a really bad financial bind at the moment. If I don't get a major influx of cash, I could lose my condo and my business. At this point I'd be willing to do just about anything." She sputtered a nervous laugh.

Reba studied her for a moment. She folded her hands on top of the desk. "I see." She continued to stare at Danielle so long and hard that she would have sworn that Reba was going to tell her she knew exactly why she was there.

A line of perspiration trickled down her back.

"I'm sorry," Danielle finally said. "I probably shouldn't have come here. You run a business and there's no reason to get you involved in my personal drama." She stood.

"No, wait. I think we can do business. How much money are you looking to make?"

"As much as possible and as quickly as possible. I'll do whatever."

"Are you sure about that?"

"I'm desperate."

"I'll have to do some checking, but I think I have the perfect opportunity. Give me a day or two to get back to you."

"Thank you so much," Danielle said profusely. Her time had just about run out, and she knew this may be her last chance inside this office. Tapping the phone didn't appear to be an option. The only other alternative was to plant a listening device somewhere in the office. She stuck her hand in her pocket and felt the tiny disk. She palmed it and stood, then quickly walked to the other side of the room to look up at the picture of Reba with the newest presidential hopeful.

"I still can't believe that's not really him."

Reba came up behind her. "That's why my business works."

Danielle spun toward her. "I better get going." She stuck out her hand, which Reba shook. "Thanks for talking to me. I'm eager to get started."

"So am I."

Danielle crossed the room to get her purse, and the instant Reba's back was turned, she stuck the recording disk beneath her desk and hoped that the signal would be strong enough to pick up something worthwhile. She straightened and walked to the door where Reba was waiting.

"Thanks again."

"You'll be hearing from me shortly."

"Great." She sucked in a breath and walked out.

The instant she was outside, she called Nick. "Well?" she said instead of hello.

"Got it all. Every angle."

"Did you get good shots of Reba?"

"Definitely."

"It was really kinda creepy seeing folks that are so recognizable but are simply look-alikes."

"Guess there are plenty of twins out there."

"And according to Reba she can help you make a mint for that very reason. I'll see you soon."

By the time she got home, Nick had already printed out the images that were taken with the miniature camera. "I still have no idea what Jenna and Anthony look like, but Mia does. They may be in one of these pictures, and if so, the connection is made." She turned to Nick and winked. "I need to get these pictures over to Mia so she can take a look at them."

"Mind if I ride with you?" His dark eyes raked over her.

Their gazes connected in a way that they hadn't before, seeing each other through different eyes in a new and different light.

She wrapped her arms around his neck and wiggled onto his lap. "I'd love nothing better," she whispered against his mouth before trailing the tip of her tongue tantalizingly across his lips.

He took her mouth in a long, slow kiss, pulled her closer, pressing her breasts against his chest. Danielle moaned ever so softly, running her fingers through his hair and pulling him deeper into the kiss.

With great reluctance he pulled back. "Keep this up and we won't be getting anywhere near Mia's house anytime soon."

She reached down and massaged the bulge in his pants. "That's the point." She gave him a devilish grin. "Mia can wait," she said, her voice thick with growing need. "But I can't."

* * *

More than two hours later, sexually satisfied and showered, they were on their way to Mia's house.

"Woman, if I knew you'd give it to me like that, I would have signed up for this spy stuff a long time ago. My legs are still shaking."

"I've been wanting to do it standing up against the wall for a while." She turned to glance at him. "But I suddenly felt the urge to be a little naughty. I got so turned on with this whole new vibe going on between us. I can't explain it."

"I can. It's about being open and trusting someone completely. Opens a whole new world. But you're right, working together like this on something a little illicit, a little dangerous, is a serious rush." His eyes narrowed. "I've always loved to watch you work, but this is different."

"I know. Just imagine if I had a gun."

They both laughed.

Shortly after, they pulled up in front of Mia's building.

"Don't forget—you don't know anything. You just took the ride to keep me company."

"Not to worry."

They hopped out of the car and went inside.

"Do you two always look so happy?" Mia asked as she ushered them inside.

"As often as we can," Nick said, hugging Danielle around the waist.

"Steve is in the living room watching something sports related," Mia said.

"Say no more." Nick headed toward the sound of screaming fans.

"So what do you have?" Mia asked, taking Danielle into the kitchen.

Danielle sat down and took out the envelope with the pictures. She spread them on the table.

"Do you recognize anyone? I mean, anyone you actually know—like Jenna and Anthony."

Mia peered and squinted at the pictures.

"Mia! For heaven's sake, would you please put on your glasses?"

Mia huffed, went over to the sink and took her eyeglass case from the shelf. She flounced back over to the table and began looking at the pictures, tossing them aside one by one. Then she stopped and looked closer at a group picture. She pointed at a couple standing behind a short woman with steel-gray hair.

"That's Jenna and Anthony."

"Are you sure?"

"Positive."

Danielle blew out a breath of relief. "That's the connection. Somehow the three of them are working this thing together."

"How are you going to prove it?"

"You're going to get me inside their house."

Chapter 21

"That's the plan, Nick," Danielle said as they lay in bed that night. "You said you wanted to help. I can't risk being the one to go over there and run into Reba."

"Does Mia know what's going on? I mean, really going on? Is she a member, too?"

"No." At least that part wasn't a lie. "She's not a member, and she only knows as much as she needs to."

He nuzzled her hair. "Hmm. Well, you know where to reach me. I'll be at the JCPenney studio tomorrow going over the designs for photographing."

"Right. I need to monitor Reba's office conversations until Mia can do her thing. Then I can get in there and grab what I need to take them all down."

Suddenly, he turned her onto her back and stared down into her eyes. A wicked smile bloomed across his mouth. "Humph, I love it when you talk dirty."

They both laughed until they were locked together in the oldest dance known to humankind.

Mia opened up her database and located Jenna and Anthony's number and dialed.

"Good morning, this is Mia Turner. Is Mrs…"

"Mia, hi—it's Jenna."

"Jenna! Hi, I'm so glad I got you on the phone. I know it's been ages since we've spoken. How have you been?"

"Fabulous. We just got back from Mexico earlier in the week. What about you? Planning any more fabulous events?"

Mia vaguely remembered that *fabulous* was Jenna's catchphrase for anything even remotely interesting.

"I've been great. Actually that's part of the reason for my call."

"I'm all ears."

"I was hoping that you'd be willing to do me a major favor."

"For you, no problem. Our circle of friends are still talking about that fabulous yacht party you put together."

Mia smiled with pride. That was certainly a signature event. Then her smile waned. At the time she didn't know she was dealing with a criminal. And even now, talking to Jenna, it was hard to believe that she could possibly be involved in something so despicable. What if she did what Danielle asked and Jenna was actually innocent? It could get back to her other clients and her business would be ruined. She'd be finished in New York, the city she'd built her business and reputation on.

"So what can I do for you?"

Mia hesitated. She could always tell Dani that she couldn't reach Jenna. Dani was obviously resourceful; she'd figure out something.

"Mia, are you still there?"

"Oh, yes, I'm sorry. I thought I was multitasking, but obviously I wasn't." She laughed nervously.

"You said you had a favor to ask. What is it?"

She drew in a long breath. "I was wondering if you would mind being part of…."

"Oh, thank you, girl," Danielle said when Mia called later that morning.

"It's all set for tomorrow at three."

"Thanks. Couldn't have pulled it off without you. You're the best."

Mia heard the relief in Danielle's voice, and whatever whispering doubts she'd had vanished. She wouldn't trade her friendship for all the business in Manhattan.

"That's what friends are for. Keep me posted. I have a meeting in twenty minutes. Gotta go."

"I'll call you tonight."

While Nick was off at the JCPenney studio, she spent the morning listening to Reba's office chatter. There was no doubt that she had a boatload of clients. But what she needed to hear was anything that would incriminate her in any way. She set the device to record when her cell phone rang.

"Hi, Dani, I didn't want to risk calling the house phone and get Nick." It was Bernard.

"Yes, he might get a little curious if you asked to

speak to me instead of him," she said, her voice light and teasing.

"What did you wind up doing with that lead I gave you?" he asked.

"We're working it as we speak."

"We?"

She squeezed her eyes shut at her flub but realized that if they were going to pull this off, she was going to need his help and Claudia's. She told him the plan they'd worked out.

"Sounds like it can work. You know this is really going to piss off Jean."

"I know. I'm sure I'll be an afterthought when this is all over, but I had a choice to make—risk my assignment or my relationship. I found a workable compromise. He only knows what he needs to know."

"Then things must be pretty good between you and Nick now?"

"Better than good, actually."

"So you two talked?"

"What do you mean?"

"Never mind. I shouldn't have butted in. I'm sure Nick will talk to you when the time is right."

"Is there something I need to know?"

"Forget that I said anything."

"Too late now, Bernard. Can you at least tell me what it's about?"

"All I will say is that it's about his past. Something that happened to him and he's never been able to let it go."

Danielle was quiet while going over a host of scenarios about what it could possibly be.

"Don't say that I mentioned anything. Let him tell you on his own."

"I won't."

"Good. Give me a call when you have something."

"I will." She disconnected the call. Nick was the one who was so intense about being honest. Was that all just a crock of crap to put the guilt trip on her? If he was so in love with her, as he claimed, why could he tell Bernard his cold, dark secret and not her?

For the same reason she'd kept her own hurts and insecurities tucked away from probing eyes, the little voice in her head whispered.

She sighed. When this was all over, she and Nick were going to have to talk, really talk. She switched her attention to the conversation that Reba was having.

Danielle sat up straight. Reba was talking to Jenna and making plans to meet to discuss the next job. The call ended but Danielle knew no more than she had before the conversation started, other than confirming that Jenna and Reba actually knew each other. And now, for whatever reason, there was some kind of job coming up. That could mean anything.

She typed up her report, as sketchy as it was, and sent an encrypted e-mail to Jean.

"Honey, I'm home," Nick called out with laughter in his voice.

When she heard him, all the gloom and doom she'd felt about their relationship vanished. They both had their issues, their baggage, and it was going to take time to unpack everything. If he could go along with the craziness that was now her life and actually want to be a part of it, then they could certainly work out anything.

She got up from the bed and walked to the front of the house.

"You're back early." She came up to him and kissed him lightly.

"I decided to bring home the breakdown and work on it here."

"Is that really the reason, or did you think you might get left out of the action?" she teased him.

"Wellll." He drew the word out and grinned. "Anything exciting happen while I was gone?"

"Not really." She told him about the one-sided conversation she'd heard at Reba's office. "But we really need to go over what we're going to do tomorrow. We definitely can't make any mistakes. And I need you to get in and get out."

"I know, I know. Don't worry. Everything will be fine. You'll see."

Chapter 22

"All you have to do is get these hidden in the bedroom and living room. They'll pick up everything that's said. I don't want you to risk tapping the phone. But if you can, use this one," Danielle instructed, holding up a third device that looked like a black dime.

"I got it, I got it," Nick said and kissed her forehead. "Don't worry. And I'll even take some pictures while I'm at it."

"I just don't want you to get caught. We don't know what they're capable of."

"Everything is going to be fine. I better get going." He pulled her close for a soft kiss. "See you soon."

Nick arrived at the condominium on East 72nd Street. The doorman Danielle had mentioned was standing in front of the building. Nick called Danielle.

"I'm here," he said. "As soon as I'm done, I'll call you."

"Okay, good luck. And, Nick…"

"Yes?"

"I… Good luck."

"Thanks."

He grabbed his bag from the passenger seat, hopped out and locked the car.

"Morning," he said, greeting the doorman.

"Good morning. Who are you here to see?"

"Mr. and Mrs. Taylor."

"Are they expecting you?"

"Yes."

Nick followed the doorman to the front desk, where he called upstairs to the Taylors.

"You can go right up," he said, hanging up the house phone. "Apartment 2710."

"Thanks." Nick sauntered off. The first hurdle was over, he thought as he stepped aside to let a young man and his miniature terrier off the elevator. The big test was ahead.

He got off on the twenty-seventh floor and walked down the hushed hallway until he reached 2710. He pressed the buzzer.

Several moments later the door was answered by a stunning redhead who introduced herself as Mrs. Taylor.

"Nick Mateo."

"Please come in. And do call me Jenna," she said. "This is so exciting. Mia is such a wonderful woman. I was surprised that she thought of me," she continued, talking as she led him inside. "And remind me again why the young lady that Mia and Reba mentioned couldn't be here."

They entered an expansive sitting room that over-looked the Manhattan skyline. The furnishings were all in white, with low glass and gold-trimmed tables topped by glorious exotic flowers in crystal vases.

"Danielle was very disappointed that she couldn't make it, but she had a last-minute assignment come up. Hope you don't mind me," he added, turning on the charm.

Jenna blushed, her pale cheeks brightening. "Of course not. What red-blooded woman would mind having a handsome young man in her home?"

Nick grinned. "You're going to make an excellent subject," he said, looking deep into her green eyes.

Jenna stood straighter. "You certainly know what to say, don't you?"

"Only the truth." He walked around the space. "I'd love to get a few shots of this room before I get started with you and your husband, if you don't mind."

"Of course not. Can I offer you something to drink?"

"No, thanks. I'm fine." He began unpacking his bag.

"While you get set up, I'll go and check what's taking my husband so long."

"Sure."

The instant she left the room, Nick placed the first listening device beneath the table near the couch. That was when he spotted the phone. He hesitated. Should he take a chance?

He listened for voices coming his way. Quickly he took off the back of the phone and placed the disk inside the phone housing next to the battery, as Danielle had showed him.

He heard Jenna's voice drawing closer. He slid the covering back on and replaced the phone only moments before she returned, with her husband in tow. He grabbed his camera and began adjusting the lens just as the couple came through the archway.

"Nick, this is my husband, Anthony. Sweetheart, this is the photographer that is going to photograph us."

Anthony Taylor stepped forward. He was about sixty, Nick estimated, and was solidly built, had a full head of salt-and-pepper hair and sharp brown eyes. He stuck out his hand.

"Pleasure to meet you. My wife told me that we are to be subjects for an article on Manhattanites."

"Yes. Ms. Holloway was commissioned to do the project. And her mutual friend, Mia Turner, suggested you."

Anthony studied Nick for so long, that Nick began to feel as if the man could see right through his lie.

"I was telling your wife that I wanted to get some shots of the room first, and probably the rest of the house, before I take your photos. Some will be posed. Others I'd like more spontaneous."

Anthony checked his wristwatch. "How long do you think this will take? I have an appointment at five."

"I promise to do this as quickly as possible."

Anthony nodded. He turned to his wife. "Call me when you're ready. I have some calls to make. Nice to meet you," he said to Nick.

"This should take about twenty minutes, and then we

can get started," Nick was saying, but Anthony was already walking away.

"Don't mind my husband," Jenna said, walking up to Nick, a little too close for his taste. "He can be a bit abrupt at times."

"I'm sure he's simply a busy man."

She stepped a bit closer and he could smell her soft but expensive-smelling perfume. Her green eyes sparkled.

Nick forced a smile and took a step back. "I should get started."

"Certainly. Mind if I watch?"

"Not at all." He adjusted his camera and began taking shots of the room from several angles, finishing up several moments later. "Can I see the rest of the house?"

"Of course." She led him through the eight-room suite, and Nick took photos of each of the exquisite spaces.

"This is an incredible place," he said, shooting the final shots of the small home theater, all the while looking for other opportunities to set up the other device that he had in his pocket. He wanted it in a room that was frequented by both of them and where conversations took place, ideally the master bedroom.

"Thank you. And last but not least is the master bedroom."

The room was incredible to behold. One wall consisted of nothing but glass looking out onto the East River beyond. A lush melon-colored rug covered the center of the floor. An enormous king-size canopied bed dominated the room.

Nick walked over to the bed and casually set down his camera on the nightstand, then made a show of looking around. "I definitely want to get this room from the right angle." He returned to the nightstand, keeping his back to Jenna, and casually placed the disk under the lip of the nightstand. Turning back, he said, "A few shots and then I can get started with you and your husband."

A little more than an hour later, Jenna was escorting Nick to the door.

"Thanks so much for your time. As soon as we get the contact sheet done, I'm sure Danielle will be in touch to go over the photos with you."

"You won't be back?" she asked in a plaintive voice.

"Depends on my schedule."

"Well," she said, lowering her voice and touching his hand, "if you ever have some free time…you have my number."

"I'll keep that in mind. Nice to meet you…and your husband," he added with meaning.

She didn't miss a beat. "Oh, Anthony is *very* understanding."

"Have a good day and thanks again," Nick said, feeling that she would undress him right at the door if he gave her half a chance. He hoisted his bag on his shoulder and returned to the elevator.

As soon as he got behind the wheel of the car, he called Danielle. "Done," he said. "I'm on my way home."

Chapter 23

By the time Nick returned, Danielle was already tapped into the Taylors' home. She waved Nick into the bedroom.

She was seated in front of the computer with a headset on. Nick joined her on the side of the bed. She turned to him.

"We got 'em," she said. "I've been recording since you called me. The husband was on the phone with Reba. They were making plans for another gathering. Apparently, Reba uses her look-alikes to gain access to people's homes and parties, and that's when their IDs are lifted, everything from passports to driver's licenses. He told her he had her money for her and would meet her later in the week."

"Wow. Have you heard anything from Reba?"

"Not yet, but I told her how desperate I was to get some extra money. I hope that will be enticing enough."

Nick turned to her. "Thanks for trusting me to do this, Dani."

She stroked his strong jaw. "That's what it's all about, right? Trust?" She searched his eyes.

He leaned forward and kissed her. "It's everything." He paused and gazed downward, then at her. "I've been wanting to talk to you about some things for a while. The time never seemed right."

"What things?"

"About me…."

By the time he finished telling her about his father and the effect it had on him, tears were streaming down Danielle's cheeks. The idea that he'd been carrying this around with him all these years and feeling that he wasn't worthy of being happy tore at her heart. Nick was the most giving, most loving man she'd ever met. He deserved happiness and he deserved to be loved as no other man she'd ever known.

"Nick…" she choked out. "I didn't know."

"It's not something that I'm proud of. But sometimes the weight of it is so heavy I can barely breathe," he said, his voice growing thick.

"There was no way you could have changed what happened. And I can't imagine that your father would have wanted you to live your life filled with guilt about what happened to him. He couldn't have. He loved you."

Nick's eyes filled. "I know. I tell myself that, but that hole never seemed to fill." His throat moved up and down but no more words came.

She wanted to say the words she knew would make it okay. But she couldn't. They just hung in her throat. Instead she said, "It will be okay. We'll get through it together." She gazed into his eyes and saw the flicker of hope there. Leaning forward, she tenderly touched her lips to his. "I promise," she whispered.

He pulled her toward him just as the phone rang. They both sighed. Danielle reached for the phone.

"Hello? Reba!" Her gaze shot to Nick. "What do I need to do?" She listened in a mixture of shock and relief. "Fine. Tomorrow. I'll be there." Slowly she hung up the phone.

"Well, what did she say?"

"She said that the people I was assigned to photograph would meet me tomorrow and my money woes would be over. I need to contact Bernard. He'll know what to do from here."

She called Bernard and brought him up to date. He told her what to do and that if she followed his instructions this would all be over by tomorrow.

"Can you hear me?" Danielle asked as she parked across the street from Jenna and Anthony's condo.

"Loud and clear. Now remember, let them do the talking. All you want to do is ask questions," Bernard instructed.

"Right." Her hands shook ever so slightly as she turned off the car. She reached for her purse and got out. "Here we go," she said into the mic taped to her chest and went into the building.

"Danielle, please come in." Jenna gave her a widening smile when she answered the buzzer.

"Thank you." She stepped inside and was both surprised and secretly delighted to see that Reba was there as well, seated next to Anthony.

Reba stood up and greeted her with a big smile. "Danielle." She turned to Anthony. "Didn't I tell you she looked liked Alicia Keys. I know we can make that work for us."

"Please have a seat," Jenna entreated.

"As I told you on the phone, Jenna and Anthony…help people. Sometimes with a new life or simply by providing them with the financial means to do so."

"I don't understand."

"It's quite simple, really," Anthony said. "We acquire property, cash, credit, homes by accessing other people's information."

Danielle feigned confusion. "Other people's information?"

"Yes, almost like a witness protection program," Reba joked. Everyone but Danielle laughed at her little quip. "All for a fee, of course, and a few favors from time to time."

"We've accessed the information from someone who would be perfect for you," Anthony said. He opened a folder that was on the table. In it was a passport and what looked to be a credit card. "You can start your new life when you walk out of this door."

Danielle looked from one calm face to other. "I just start a new life as—" she looked at the name on the license "—Michelle Ingram."

"Yes, let's say that Ms. Ingram is out of the picture."

Danielle's heart thumped. "What do I need to do, I mean, you said, 'for a fee,'" she said, turning to Reba.

Reba smiled broadly. "We get a portion of the proceeds, which is how we continue to finance others who need our services and live the lifestyles to which we've grown accustomed." They all laughed.

There was a sudden loud bang, and the front door burst open. Bernard rushed in, followed by Claudia and a man Danielle didn't recognize, all with guns in hand.

Anthony leaped up.

"Don't even move," Claudia said.

"We've been watching you for a while," Bernard said as he went behind Anthony to put on plastic cuffs.

"I lot of people are going to be very happy to get their *real* lives back," Claudia said.

"There must be some mistake!" Jenna insisted.

"Take your hands off me," Reba shouted to the man who put her hands behind her back.

"Oh, there's no mistake," Bernard said, pulling out a tape recorder from the breast pocket of his jacket. He pressed Play and the damning conversation of moments ago filled the room for all to hear.

Jenna shot Danielle a murderous look. "I was a fool to trust you."

"I think it best that you keep your comments to yourself," Danielle said, suddenly feeling brave. "You're in enough trouble."

"Yes, and you will have plenty of years to think about it," Claudia added, shoving Anthony toward the door.

The cuffed trio was led out by Bernard and the third man.

Claudia turned to Danielle. "Are you okay?"

Danielle nodded, still shaken by the events of the past few minutes.

"You did a great job, Dani. You should be proud of yourself."

"I guess I will be when my heart slows down." She sputtered a nervous laugh.

Claudia grinned. "You'll get used to it. Come on, help me round up their computer and files."

"Who was that other guy with you and Bernard?"

Claudia grinned. "Oh, just a good friend of the family."

Chapter 24

Later that night, Nick and Danielle were in the tub with bubbles up to their necks, drinking wine and listening to a jazz CD.

Nick stroked Danielle beneath the water, and she squirmed in delight. "We're supposed to be relaxing, getting rid of stress," she teased.

"I am getting rid of stress. Can't you tell?" He caressed her breasts. "Are you ever going to tell me everything, about this organization?" he asked.

"If I could, I would. I've already messed up big-time by getting you involved. What I can tell you is that there may be times in my life and parts of it that I can't share with you. And it's not because I don't trust you or that I don't…love you."

"You what?"

She felt his heart pound against her back. She turned in the tub, coming up on her knees so that she faced him. "Love you," she repeated. "I love you."

"Do you really mean that?"

"From the bottom of my heart." And for the first time in her life, that enormous weight was lifted from her spirit. She had a man who loved her through thick and thin, not based on what she looked like or felt about herself but because of who she was, the woman she'd become.

"If we love each other, Dani, we can get through anything...even this spy stuff."

She leaned forward, linked her fingers behind his head. "I knew I loved you for a reason," she murmured before slowly lowering herself onto his erection. "There are some people I want you to meet," she said, moving slowly against him.

"Who?"

"My parents. I think you'll really like them, and I know they'll love you as much as I do."

The following morning Danielle received a call from Jean requesting that she come to the brownstone as soon as possible.

"If tomorrow afternoon works, I'll be there," Danielle said. "I have some business to take care of and it can't wait."

"I know," Jean said. "I'll be waiting." She disconnected the call and Danielle shook her head in wonder. What didn't that woman know?

The last time Danielle had been to this house was nearly ten years earlier. She'd walked away and never looked back, building her life of make-believe and blaming her parents for everything that was wrong in her life and with her.

She was a big girl now, a full-grown woman who had to finally face her own demons and own up to the hurt that she'd caused over the years.

Sure, she'd kept in touch at all the appropriate times over the years, with cards or phone calls, but this was different.

Nick clasped her hands and forced her to look at him. "It's going to be all right. I promise. Parents don't stop loving their children. And I have a gut feeling they're going to be so happy to see you that all the years apart are going to melt away." He gave her a lopsided grin and her heart thumped.

She swallowed over the dry knot in her throat and nodded her head.

"Come on, let's do this," Nick said, opening the car door, then coming around to open hers. He helped her out of the car and pulled her close. "Tell me again," he whispered against her mouth.

"I love you, Nick Mateo, with all my heart."

"Damn, I love the sound of that." He pecked her softly on the lips, and they walked toward the blue-and-white framed house.

Before they reached the front door, it opened and her parents stood in the archway.

For an instant no one moved. And then all at once her parents swept her up in their joined embrace, kissing and hugging their prodigal daughter.

Nick stepped aside and let them have their private moment. Finally Danielle turned, her expression luminous. Her eyes sparkled with tears.

"Mom, Dad, this is Nick Mateo."

Nick stepped forward with a big grin on his face.

Danielle's father stuck out his hand. "Pleasure to meet you."

"You as well, Mr. Holloway."

"Call me Joe."

"Well, are we going to continue this reunion on the steps, or are you young people going to come inside?" her mother, Carmen, asked, beaming at them both.

Several happy hours later, Danielle and Nick were on their way back to Manhattan.

"So this is where you grew up?" Nick asked as they rode through stately St. Albans, Queens.

"Yep, and I used to play right in that park on Saturday afternoons," Danielle said, pointing to Addisleigh Park. "There was always something going on, concerts, tournaments." She smiled at the memories.

"Your folks are great." He glanced at her face for a moment. "You have your dad's eyes," he said softly, "and his strong-willed personality," he added.

Danielle laughed. "That much is true." And for the first time that she could remember in years she loved the sound of that.

"You don't know how lucky you are to still have a dad that loves you as much as yours does," he said wistfully.

"You did, too." She squeezed his hand. "And just because he's not here physically doesn't mean that the love he had for you wasn't real. You'll always carry that in your heart. And," she added, "now you have mine to love you, too."

He turned to her and smiled. "I like the sound of that."

"Yeah, me, too."

As they continued the drive home in a comforting silence, Danielle thought about her father's parting words as he hugged her.

"I told you a long time ago, sweetheart, that one day you would find someone who would love you for who you were, not who you appeared to be. You found him," he'd said, smiling softly. "Be sure to take care of him. Real love often only comes once in a lifetime."

"I love you, Daddy," she whispered, hugging him tight.

He kissed the top of her silky hair. "I know, sweetheart. I've always known."

Danielle sighed deeply, leaned back against the headrest and closed her eyes. Her father had been right all along. And if it took the rest of her life, she would ensure that her mom and dad never doubted her love for them ever again.

Chapter 25

Danielle sat straight as an arrow in the chair facing Jean. The look on Jean's face was so hard that Danielle would have bet money it would have cracked had she opened her mouth.

Jean turned her hard gaze on Danielle. "You did an incredible job on your first assignment. You used your instincts. I like that."

Danielle was so stunned she couldn't speak.

"Because of you, a major operation has been dismantled. My clients are happy and Bernard now has the information he needs to take out the next level. You should be proud."

"Thank you."

"But you broke every rule of the Cartel. You allowed

your personal life to get involved. People could have gotten hurt. Fortunately, it worked out. It seems that you and Savannah have a way of breaking the rules and making this work for you." She handed Danielle a folder. "See if you can handle this one. And, Danielle…"

"Yes, ma'am."

"Try to keep the Cartel out of your bedroom next time."

"Yes, ma'am."

Danielle emerged from the brownstone walking on air. She'd accomplished much more than this assignment. Not only had she exposed those who worked to steal the lives and livelihoods of others, but also she'd found herself in the process. All these years she'd been searching for her own identity, hiding behind the lens of a camera, and she now finally knew without a doubt who she was—Joe and Carmen Holloway's daughter. That was what really made her proudest.

Mia and Savannah were waiting for her on the sidewalk in front of the brownstone. She greeted them with a broad grin.

"Well?" they asked in unison.

Danielle wrapped her arms around her two dearest friends in the world.

"I have so much to tell you both."

"Good stuff, I hope," Savannah said as they walked hand in hand toward Danielle's vehicle.

They all climbed in.

"I took Nick to meet my parents," she began as she started the engine.

Mia gave her a knowing look, which Savannah caught.

"What am I missing?" Savannah asked.

Danielle drew in a breath and eased out into traffic. "A long time ago, there was this guy named Michael…."

By the time they'd reached The Shop, Danielle had concluded her sad and sordid tale of her relationship gone terribly wrong.

"Dani, my God, you've been carrying that around all these years," Savannah said as they were shown their seats at their favorite booth. "I knew you and your folks weren't close, but I had no idea."

"Yeah, and I let it make a mess of my life, cut off my parents and harden my heart. I've been so scared of falling in love again, of being ashamed of who I was, that I nearly lost everything in the process."

"But you didn't," Mia said.

"And now you have Nick," Savannah said.

Danielle grinned. "Yes, I do. He still doesn't know everything about the Cartel, but he said that as long as we love each other, we can work anything out. And none of that changed after he met my folks."

"So it's finally official?" Mia asked with a gleam in her eye. "You're in love and not afraid to admit it!"

Danielle smiled. "And it feels damned good. If I learned one thing through all this, it's that you have to be who you are. Accept yourself for who you are. And sticking labels and tags on people only separates you from them because underneath it all we're just people. And living a lie, a life of pretense, can only hurt you and everyone who cares about you."

"I'll drink to that," Savannah said, raising her glass of water.

The trio toasted to love and friendship.

"Ladies, lunch is on me!" Danielle announced.

"And I'll drink to that," Mia said.

When Danielle returned to her apartment later that evening, she couldn't remember the last time she'd felt so good about herself and the possibilities of the future.

She had a dream job, parents who loved her and the photo assignment of a lifetime, and when things got dull, she always had the Cartel. But most important, she had Nick.

She dropped her purse on the hall table and headed toward the bedroom, where she heard the sound of the television. Her heart skipped a beat just thinking about seeing Nick.

She opened the bedroom door; Nick was propped up on pillows watching the news.

"Hey, babe," Nick greeted her. He pointed to the screen. "They were just talking about a major identity theft ring that had been broken up. Thousands of people's personal information was recovered, but it's still going to take months to unravel everything."

Danielle came and sat next to him.

"Just think, you helped to pull that off." He hugged her tightly.

She snuggled next to him. "With your help."

He grinned. "Yeah, how 'bout that. So how was lunch with the girls?"

"Great. We were talking about planning Claudia and

Bernard's wedding. She wants a fall wedding, which doesn't give us much time, but I think we can put together something really spectacular."

"Now that we've got our own hurdles out of the way," he began slowly, "there's no reason why we shouldn't."

Danielle frowned. "Shouldn't what?"

Nick disentangled himself and got up from the bed. He paced in front of her for a moment.

"Nick…what is it?"

He knelt down in front of her and took her hands in his. "I've been doing a lot of thinking… especially since we went to meet your parents."

Her heart thumped. *Here it comes,* she thought and didn't want to hear the rest, not after she'd finally opened her heart and soul. Not now. She couldn't breathe.

"Will you marry me, Danielle?"

For a hot minute she didn't process what he'd said. "What?"

"Will you marry me? Will you be my wife and have our beautiful babies, be my best friend through thick and thin, make a life with me? Say yes, Dani."

Her spirit was so filled with awe and joy that the words wouldn't come. She cupped his face in her hands and looked deeply into his eyes.

"There's nothing in this world that I want more," she finally said, her voice thick and shaky with emotion.

Nick dug into his jeans pocket and pulled out a black velvet box. He opened the top and a sparkling diamond winked back at her. It was a simple setting, nothing fancy, but nothing was more beautiful.

He took her hand and slipped the ring on her finger.

Tears of joy spilled from her eyes.

"I hope those are happy tears," he said.

"Yes, yes, yes!" She pulled him to her, and they tumbled onto the bed, giddy with joyous laughter.

"I guess you girls will be planning two weddings," Nick said as he slowly undressed her.

"Absolutely." And she sealed her promise with a kiss.

* * * * *

We hope you enjoyed reading
SEDUCTION AND LIES.
The following is an excerpt from
TEMPTATION AND LIES, the next book
in the exciting TLC *series by Donna Hill.*
This book will be on sale February 2009
at bookstores everywhere.

Chapter 1

The October sun peeked through the slats in the vertical blinds throwing a soft glow across Mia's state-of-the-art kitchen. Mia loved to cook and considered herself somewhat of a gourmet chef always willing to try new recipes. And she firmly believed that a good meal opened and soothed the soul. The best conversations, confessions and gossip could be had over a good meal.

With her piping hot mug of imported Turkish coffee on the left, her sparkling, pearl-handled .22 on the right, she snapped open *The Daily News* and immediately turned to Page Six. She circled several high-profile items about celebs and business tycoons spotted in and an around The Big Apple as she sipped her coffee. The smooth blend had been a gift from one of her grateful clients. She made a note on the pad next to her saucer to call Paul Han and thank him for his "thank you."

Page Six aside, she turned her attention to the egg-white omelet that she painstakingly prepared every morning. It was stuffed with mushrooms, tomatoes, green peppers and cheddar cheese. She took a forkful and sighed with pleasure.

There were two things that were paramount in Mia's life: great food and paying clients. Well, three things—order. No, make that four—Steven.

The last item on her must-have list made her smile. Her best friends Savannah Fields and Danielle Hollo-way teased her about her neurotic obsessions, but they had to agree that Steven Long was certainly worth being obsessed about.

Mia was the last of the trio to find someone special in her life. Savannah and Blake had been married for seven years and just had their first child—Mikayla—the most gorgeous baby girl the world had ever seen. And Danielle had finally allowed her heart to open and let Nick Mateo in and they were now living together and engaged!

For a while Mia believed she'd always be the fifth wheel. Until she'd actually taken a second look at Steven Long.

They'd known each other casually for years, as Blake and Steven were best friends and business partners at their architectural and development company.

But it wasn't until Mia hosted a party at her house about ten months earlier that they actually "saw" each other as more than "the best friend of their best friend." Since that night, Mia and Steven had been pretty much inseparable, only allowing the pressing business of their respective livelihoods to keep them apart.

Mia closed her paper, finished off her omelet and washed it down with the last of her coffee.

She took her dishes to the sink, rinsed then placed them in the dishwasher.

This part of her morning ritual completed, she took her gun from the table and walked the short hallway that led from the front of the two-bedroom condo to the back where the master bedroom and reconverted second bedroom was located.

She and Steven used that second bedroom as their combined office, so she would never risk him discovering the contents of her "kit," as Danielle's lover, Nick, had done.

A minor disaster like that would take more explaining than she was willing to do. So being the orderly and forward-thinking type-A personality that she was, Mia had cut out a little panel behind the top shelf of her clothes closet, hidden behind boxes of very expensive shoes.

She removed the panel and pulled out her TLC "beauty kit." Mia smiled as she ran her hand across the smooth pink leather carrying case with the TLC logo emblazoned across the front.

Taking the case to the bed, she turned the latch to review the contents: burglary tools, computer scanning disk, listening and recording devices, chloroform and a fingerprint dusting kit and of course the container that held the bath beads which were really specially designed tranquilizer bullets for her .22. All of the contents were ingeniously camouflaged as bath oil, body lotions, eye shadows, blush, perfumes and lipsticks. She smiled.

Assured that everything was in order and accounted for, she lifted the top tray and replaced the gun in its cutout compartment below. She knew it was risky to take the gun out each morning after Steven was gone for work, but the thrill of seeing it right next to her, where she could admire and stroke it, even though it only held tranquilizer bullets—it still gave her a rush.

Mia had become an official member of the Cartel seven months earlier, although she'd been a fringe member since Savannah's first case a little more than a year ago, which turned up an ugly land deal that would have destroyed an ancient African burial ground right in downtown Brooklyn.

As the owner and CEO of NT Management, Mia's schedule, though hectic, was her own. That flexibility lent itself to her sideline as an undercover operative for TLC.

Mia returned her kit to its hiding place and checked the time. Jean Armstrong, the head of the Cartel, had requested that Mia come to the Harlem brownstone to discuss a new assignment that Jean felt Mia was perfect for.

From there it would be off to her real job—the one she could tell everyone about, she thought with a smile.

Event management was the perfect occupation for Mia. It gave her the opportunity to arrange every aspect of an event down to the most mundane detail—and she loved every minute of it.

Ever since she was a little girl, growing up in Bedford Stuyvesant in Brooklyn, she'd had a knack for arrang-

ing things. As a preschooler she had a precise time and
location for all of her doll tea parties and all of the accessories had to match and be placed "just so" on the
tiny pink plastic table.

She remembered the most traumatic incident in her
young life was when she went to place the teacups on
the saucers and discovered that one of the handles was
broken and there were no more in her collection that
matched. "You see, the tablecloth, paper napkins and the
dolls' outfits were all color-coordinated," she'd explained to Savannah and Danielle many years later,
who'd both given her sympathetic looks.

She'd become so hysterical that her mother had to
promise to replace the entire set the following day. Mia
was only five at the time, and her obsession with detail
and order only grew and crystallized as she got older.

Of course, nowadays she didn't collapse into tears
and fits, but her entire demeanor would become one
tightly wound band of tension that was terribly uncomfortable to be around.

That aside, Mia Turner was your everyday, ordinary
kind of woman. Unless, of course, you counted her
"other life."

She squinted at her appearance in the oval hall mirror.
Her smooth, shoulder-length hair haloed her face in soft
waves. The slight touches of makeup—bronze lip gloss,
mascara and a little powder to keep the shine off her
nose—kept her lovely features from being overshad-
owed. She cinched the belt on her knee-length dress,
took her coat and purse and headed out, checking the
locks three times before she felt comfortable.

* * *

Twenty minutes later she pulled onto 135th Street in Harlem. She parked her midnight-blue Lexus two doors down from the brownstone. The luxury car was a recent present to herself for having a stellar year of profits for her business. In the tight economic times, everyone was cutting back, but her business continued to flourish. Big business, celebrities and the well-off were always having conventions or hosting parties to sell something, impress others or remind everyone else how important they were, and NT Management was the one they invariably called.

Mia slid off her glasses and tucked them into her purse. Mia was terribly nearsighted but refused to wear her glasses in public and was adamant about not "sticking something in her eyes" as she put it, referring to contact lenses. So vanity won out and she went through life squinting, which often gave her a severe appearance that was totally contrary to her open and warm personality. In business, however, it often worked in her favor as in her dealings and negotiations her steely gaze gave the impression of a no-nonsense business owner.

She gathered her purse and hopped out, her chocolate-colored Manolo Blahnik ankle boots, hitting the pavement with a soft pop.

She grabbed her ecru-colored swing coat from the hook in the back of the car and quickly slipped it on. Although it was early October and the sun was high in the sky, the weather had already begun to grow cool.

Setting the alarm on the car, she headed to the brownstone and rang the bottom bell.

Within moments, Claudia, Savannah's mother, came to the door.

"Hello, darling," Claudia greeted her, enveloping Mia in a warm hug. The soft scent of Chanel floated around her.

Claudia Martin was in her early sixties but she didn't look a day over forty-five. Class and style would always be connected to Claudia. She kept her auburn-tinted hair in a fierce cut that rivaled the early Halle Berry look. Her cinnamon complexion was flawless and she rarely wore much makeup, save for a dash of lipstick and mascara to accentuate her incredible hazel eyes. St. John was her designer of choice, and she wore it well.

It was Claudia, a member of TLC for several years, who'd recruited her daughter Savannah. And all those years that Mia, Savannah and Danielle had seen Claudia toting around her TLC carry-all and saying she was going to meetings, they always believed what she told them: that she was selling beauty products. Ha!

The joke between them now that Savannah had a daughter of her own was that she would recruit little Mikayla when she became of age. Knowing her already feisty infant, Savannah had said Mikayla would probably launch her own division of TLC Tots.

"Looking good as always, Claudia. Bernard must be treating you well. You're glowing."

Claudia laughed lightly. "That he does, my dear. Nothing like a good man to get the kinks out." She winked at Mia and walked inside.

"Have you two finally set a date?"

"Actually, I wanted to talk to you about that." She

clasped Mia's arm and her diamond ring flashed in the late morning light. "Now that Savannah had the baby and can fit into something 'fabulous' as she said, we wanted a December wedding. Do you think you can put something together in time?"

Mia stopped short, propped her hand on her hip and gave Claudia a look of mild reprimand. "Claudia, this is me. If you said your wedding was this afternoon and you wanted it in Paris, I would make it happen. It's what I do."

Claudia laughed in response. "Chile, what was I thinking? Go on," she said, still chuckling. "Jean is upstairs in her office."

"We'll make an appointment to talk," she promised before heading off.

Mia went up the stairs and down the "hall of fame," as it had been dubbed. The walls on either side were lined with portraits of all the Cartel members who had been a member for at least a year and had successfully completed their assignments. She smiled as she spotted Savannah's photo, and then two photos down was one of Danielle. Claudia's was at the beginning of the row, right next to Jean. Mia drew in a breath of resolve. One day soon her photo would grace the hall of fame, too.

Mia knocked lightly on the closed door.

"Come in." Jean looked up from her computer screen when Mia entered. "Have a seat. I'll be right with you."

Mia did as instructed, taking in the room while she waited. As with all of the brownstones in Harlem and in Brooklyn—that had not been cut up or reconverted—

the rooms were enormous. *Grand* would be a better word. Vaulted ceilings, crystal chandeliers, parquet floors, mahogany sliding doors, massive mantelpieces, stained-glass windows and working fireplaces. Some even had the claw-foot bathtubs and original porcelain sconces.

She'd grown up in a brownstone on Putnam Avenue in Brooklyn. Not one quite as big as this one, but large enough. So any time she came here she felt right at home.

Mia crossed her legs.

"Thank you for coming," Jean began, bypassing any pleasantries.

Mia merely nodded, knowing from experience that Jean wasn't one for chitchat.

"I have an assignment that is perfect for you, especially with the business that you're in."

Jean took a sealed manila envelope from her desk drawer. "All of the details are inside. I'll briefly give you some background. This was handed to me from a personal contact in the FBI. There are some extremely high-profile individuals involved, and before the lid gets blown off, they need to be absolutely sure." She cleared her throat and removed her pink-framed glasses, setting them gently down on the desktop. "There is a major, very elite, very exclusive escort service operating in New York City. Although that's nothing new, what is new is that it appears to be run by Avante Enterprises. You need to find a way to get inside the organization, and get the evidence that the Feds need to shut it down."

For an instant, Mia couldn't move. She hoped that

Jean couldn't read the distress on her face, or hear the escalated pounding of her heart. Avante Enterprises had been one of her clients, and several years ago she'd broken a cardinal rule and had a short but fiery affair with its CEO, Matthew Burke.

Chapter 2

Mia managed to get through the rest of the briefing without screaming. When she got behind the wheel of her Lexus she wasn't quite certain she'd heard anything Jean said after she dropped her Matthew Burke bombshell.

By rote she turned the key in the ignition. The engine purred to life along with the sounds of Marvin Gaye's classic, "What's Going On?"

That was the question of the day, she mused. She put on her glasses, drew in a long, steadying breath and slowly pulled off in the early afternoon traffic.

In the privacy of her business office, a ground-floor rental in SoHo, Mia closed and locked the door on the off chance that her new assistant, Ashley Temple, decided to burst in—as she was prone to do—to update her on the latest TMZ news (a celebrity online and off-line news outlet). She was relieved that Ashley wasn't up front when she came in and she was able to get to her office undetected, at least for the time being.

Mia depressed the "do not disturb" button on her phone then removed the manila envelope from her purse. She placed it on the desk and stared at the innocuous-looking envelope. It looked like millions of others, but she knew better. The contents had the potential to turn her life inside out.

The affair between her and Michael had been discreet. No one knew about it, especially within the business circles they traveled. Not even Savannah or Danielle had any idea that anything had transpired. They'd always believed that she simply hadn't found the right man. And until she'd met Michael, she hadn't.

When they'd broken up it was a long three years before she started intermittently dating again. But she'd never found anyone who could measure up—until Steven Long.

Mia ran her manicured finger across the smooth surface of the envelope.

If she broke the seal and opened it, there was no turning back. She'd have to carry out the assignment. Her type-A personality wouldn't allow her to give up or turn the reins over to someone else.

Drawing in a long breath, she exhaled her doubts and trepidations and broke the seal.

The documents detailed Michael's rise up the business ranks to eventually run his own management company. He was considered one of the best in the management consulting business.

Her pulse pounded in her temples when she scrolled down to review his personal information.

Marital Status: divorced.

Reflexively she gripped the pages tighter between her fingers. Her heart thumped as her breathing shortened.

Divorced. He was free. At least on paper.

He had been married when they'd met. Guilt riddled her each time they'd made love until her conscience would no longer allow her to do that to another woman. Michael had literally begged her not to leave him. He promised to get a divorce. "Just give me some time," he'd said.

But time and promises were things she could not depend on, nor did she want to.

"I can't do this anymore, Michael," she'd said to him, the agony of speaking the words making her voice paper-thin, sounding weak and without conviction.

He turned onto his side. His dark brown eyes moved slowly along her face. His thumb brushed across her bottom lip. "Do what?" he asked, his voice husky and taunting. "This?" His large hand slid between her damp thighs and gently caressed her there.

Mia drew in a sharp breath as the powerful sensations rippled through her.

"Mike…" Her hips arched. She gripped his shoulders and he rose above her, bracing his weight on his forearms.

"I love you so much, Mia," he said on a ragged breath as he pushed slowly inside her.

Mia wrapped her body and her heart around him, giving him all of her because she knew that it could never happen again.

And it didn't.

Mia ran her hand along the length of her hair and for a moment shut her eyes, wishing the images of the past away.

She looked down and read further. Michael had been under surveillance for a while. He'd come under suspicion during a routine audit of his company's finances. There were several discrepancies which were apparently cleared up, but he remained a blip on the screen.

Apparently deposits of three to five thousand dollars were routinely placed in one of his secondary accounts, then were quickly transferred to an offshore account in the Cayman Islands.

The more she read, the more ill she became.

The Michael Burke that she knew was ambitious, and he could be manipulative if it would land him an account. But this man on paper was not the man she remembered and once loved.

She closed the folder and knew that shortly the ink would disappear, as if the damning words had never existed.

The knock on her door snapped her to attention. She shoved the envelope into her desk drawer, removed her glasses and went to unlock the door.

"Hi. Come in."

Ashley's modernized Angela Davis 'fro bounced in a cinnamon-brown halo around her openly expressive face.

Mia was always reminded of a highly energetic, inquisitive child every time she looked at Ashley, even though she was easily in her early thirties.

Ashley was a godsend after Mia lost her last assistant to "marriage and happily ever after." Ashley was bright, totally efficient and loved the event planning business. She was so good, in fact, that Mia had given Ashley two of her own accounts to manage, and her clients loved her.

"Hey, boss," Ashley greeted her, her warm brown eyes sparkling as always. Her deep dimples flashed.

"What's up?"

"A couple of calls that I thought you'd want to handle personally." She handed over a slip of the company's teal-colored message paper.

They walked toward the small circular table situated in the far corner of the office and sat down.

Mia squinted at the words on the page until they came into focus. "Sahara Club?" she asked.

Ashley read from a sheet in her hand detailing all the particulars about the Sahara Club that catered to married couples that wanted to plan quick romantic getaways. The club management wanted to put together an event to advertise their business as well as invite previous guests to give testimonials about their experience.

Mia's brows rose as she listened.

"I searched them on the Internet," Ashley offered in response to the question that hovered on Mia's lips. She handed over her research material. "I also have a short list of some of their clients. I can have them checked if you want."

Mia took the notes and briefly scanned them, the words blurry around the edges.

"This one is for a grand opening of a boutique in Tribeca," Ashley went on, reading her second set of notes. "They want something really upscale. They'd like to come in and talk with you. Should I schedule it?"

"Why don't you take that one," Mia said absently. "I'll sit in on the initial meeting if you need me, but I think you can handle it."

"No problem." She paused a moment. "Are you okay? You seem really out of it."

In the six months that Ashley had worked for Mia they'd grown rather close, sharing stories and giving each other advice on things like clothes, cars, best deals, politics, religion. Mia had even invited Ashley to join her, Savannah and Danielle for their weekly girls' brunch at their favorite hangout, The Shop. Over time Mia had grown to respect Ashley's judgment and clear-headed opinions, which she often sought. But her current dilemma, she could not share.

"I'm fine. Just a little headache."

Ashley leaned forward. "Maybe if you wore your glasses to read and move around in the world, your head would stop hurting. It's probably eyestrain."

Mia made a face. It was her personal pet peeve. "I'll be fine. I'll take something for it."

Ashley huffed. "Suit yourself." She pushed up from the desk. "I'll give these ladies from the boutique a call and get that set up."

"Thanks."

Alone now, Mia's thoughts reluctantly turned to her most pressing situation: in order to fulfill her assignment, she was going to have to see Michael again. And she wasn't sure how she was going to handle that.

What she needed was some advice. Savannah was

totally out of the question. She was a devout believer in the sanctity of marriage. She'd had her own scare with her husband, Blake, and she didn't look favorably on "the other woman," which is what Mia had been.

Danielle, though much more open-minded, had mellowed since she'd settled down with Nick. And although she might be more prone to understanding, Dani's quick, sharp tongue was not something she wanted to deal with either.

Those were the reasons why she'd never told her two best friends about what had gone on between her and Michael. It went against everything that they believed in. She'd cringe every time the topic of adultery and cheating came up during one of their chats. She never wanted to disappoint them or see that appalled look in their eyes. She knew they'd demand an explanation as to why, and she wouldn't be able to provide one, because she didn't know why.

Sounds of Ashley singing a very bad rendition of a Mary J Blige tune drifted to her ears. Mia smiled. Oh, to be carefree, she mused.

Her phone rang.

"NT Management, Mia speaking."

"Hello, baby. Caught you at your desk."

"Hi, sweetie. This is a surprise. To what do I owe the pleasure?"

"I have a couple of hours and I thought I'd swing by and take my favorite girl to a late lunch. If you haven't eaten already."

"I'd love to."

"Great. See you in about twenty minutes."

"Okay." Mia hung up the phone. Spending some time with Steven was just the medicine she needed.

As promised, twenty minutes later, Steven was walking through the door.

Mia's heart skipped a beat when she saw him. She stood and came from behind her desk, her body warming with every step.

"Hi," she whispered as she came to a stop in front of him.

Steven Long was, for lack of a better word, gorgeous. His complexion was the color of polished mahogany, a hard square jaw and chocolate-brown eyes with silky brows and lashes to die for.

Two years in a row *Jet* magazine had listed him as one of New York's most eligible bachelors. That was before he'd hooked up with Mia. Now he was off the market, permanently if Mia had any say so in the matter.

His gunmetal-gray suit fit every inch of his six-foot frame and, damn, didn't she love a man in a good-looking suit. His pearl-gray shirt and burgundy-and-gray striped tie set off the suit and his skin to perfection.

Steven snaked his arm around Mia's waist and swept her into a deep, lingering kiss that took her breath away. When he released her she felt shaken and hot with desire.

"You're going to have to stop by more often," she said, stroking his cheek with the tip of her finger.

He grinned. "If only I could, gorgeous. How's your day been so far?"

Reality slammed into her. Her heart thumped. "Huh, not bad. We may have two more clients."

"That's great, congrats."

"Good for business but not great for relationships. It means that I'll be even more busy," she said, knowing that in the coming weeks she would need as much time away from Steven as necessary.

He took her hand and massaged the center of her palm in sensuous circular motions that sent shivers running through her.

"If anyone can multitask and make it look like child's play, it's you, babe." He pecked her softly on the lips. "I ain't worried," he said with a grin. "Come on, let's go before we spend all of our free time talking about what time we won't have."

"Lead the way."

"How did you manage to get time away from the office?" Mia asked as they were seated in a back booth at Brothers Bistro, a great health-food eatery within walking distance of her office.

"Blake is in the field working on some sketches of the renovation project in Brooklyn. This morning I put the finishing touches on the blueprints for the town houses in D.C. and realized I actually had some breathing room for a change."

It was amazing how far Steven and Blake had come in just over a decade. They'd built their business from a two-man company working out of a storefront to becoming one of the major players with a staff of ten, an office on Madison Avenue and contracts that were expanding their business from its Manhattan locale to the Capital.

"If business keeps growing the way it has been, any midday getaway would be wishful thinking," Steven said.

"Are you and Blake planning to hire more people?"

"We may have to just to handle the volume. But my fear is, as I've explained to Blake, at some point the bottom is going to drop out. Builders are going to stop building because no one can afford to buy."

Mia nodded in agreement. She knew all too well the fragility of the current economy and how it had wreaked havoc on countless American businesses, not to mention the thousands who'd lost homes.

"I don't want to have to hire new people and realize in six months or a year that we have to let them go."

"What does Blake say?"

"You know Blake, Mr. Optimistic, but I think I'm getting him to see my point."

"So what's plan B?"

"Work our asses off," he said with a chuckle.

Mia raised her water glass. "To working our asses off."

As she sat there laughing and talking with the man she loved and who loved her back, she knew that it was only a matter of time before the lies began. And she could only pray that he never found out—not even so much about the Cartel, which would be devastating enough—but about her affair with Michael.

Savannah's censure she could live with. Danielle's sharp tongue she could handle. But the hurt and lack of respect that she knew would be in Steven's eyes would kill her inside. She would do whatever it took to keep that information from him. She'd get through it.

But the true test would come when she saw Michael again for the first time. She knew it would be soon.

Much too soon.

Chapter Three

It had been three days since Mia received her assignment, and she had yet to do anything about it. She felt frozen, torn between what she had agreed to do—the oath she'd sworn—and the possible repercussions if she did what was necessary.

"Mia."

She glanced up from the files on her desk and was surprised to see Ashley standing in front of her.

"I…didn't hear you come in," she muttered.

"I know. I knocked three times, but you didn't answer. I've been standing here for a good thirty seconds and you didn't budge. Is everything okay? You've been totally out of it and distracted for the past few days. That's so not like you."

Mia sighed heavily and leaned back in her chair. She'd been debating about sharing some of her dilemma with Ashley—an abridged version—with the hope of getting an objective viewpoint. But because of the sensitivity of the issue she'd balked at airing her dirty laundry. But holding it in was driving her crazy.

She was a person of action, one who dealt with issues head-on. This inertia was maddening.

"You want to talk?" Ashley nudged gently. "I'm a pretty good listener," she added with an encouraging smile.

Mia pressed her lips together in thought. Finally she spoke. "Have you ever been in a situation when an old flame came back into your life?"

"Sure. Why?" She sat down on the chair besides Mia's desk.

"What did you do?"

"Well, we had dinner, talked about old times, the way things were. I spent the night at his place and we woke up the next morning and realized that it was truly over—you can't go back. At least me and Dave couldn't."

"Hmm." Mia's gaze drifted away. Spending the night with Michael was not an option. She couldn't do that to Steven in a million years.

"Is that what's going on?" Ashley tentatively asked.

Mia turned her gaze on Ashley. "Something like that. I'll put it this way, seeing him again is inevitable."

"And you don't know how to handle it."

"It's been a long time," Mia admitted. "But a lot was left unresolved."

"Well, I'd never be one to tell somebody what to do but the one thing I do know, unless you resolve whatever it is that's eating at you, it will always jump up and get in your way." She smiled softly. "You'll work it out."

Ashley hopped up from her seat. "My bill is in the mail," she teased, drawing a chuckle from Mia. "The meeting with Verve Boutique is still on for noon."

"Right, the ones from Tribeca."

"Yep. They should be here soon."

Mia nodded. "Buzz me when you're ready."

"Sure." She headed for the door then stopped. "Mia…"

"Yes?"

"Like I said, I don't give advice often, but if I can offer this one piece, just think with your head and not with your heart." She tossed up her hands. "That's it." She grinned and sauntered out.

Ashley was right, Mia thought. She was thinking and behaving on pure emotion and old memories.

Michael was more than over her by now. She was sure he'd moved on and was probably involved with someone.

She was getting bent out of shape about nothing. What she needed to concentrate on was finding a way to get the information she needed.

That thought was like a knife to the chest. The idea that Michael could be behind an escort service still had her stunned. She believed it to be impossible. But the reality was, people did change. And if that adage was true, then Michael Burke was definitely not the man she remembered.

Think with your head.

That was exactly what she was going to start doing. She swiveled her chair toward her flat-screen computer that sat on the right-hand side of her desk. She did a quick search for Avante Enterprises. Within moments a list of choices came up on the screen. She chose the link that opened the company Web site.

Michael's handsome face greeted her and her breath caught in her throat as a flood of memories rushed to the surface. *Think with your head.* She pushed the images back and started taking notes.

Before she knew it, she'd filled three pages and Ashley was buzzing her about their noon appointment. She shoved the notes in her desk. At least she'd done something concrete, she thought, mildly satisfied with herself.

She closed the file, got up from her desk and went to join the ladies in the conference space.

Felicia and Linda Hall were sisters and the proud owners of Verve. They'd been in business for about a year, but never had the grand opening that they really wanted. Now, with some experience under their belts and a solid customer base, they thought it was time.

Felicia was the talker of the duo and wasted no time laying out what they wanted: a full weekend with music, entertainment, food and plenty of media coverage, she'd said.

"What kind of budget do you have to work with?" Mia asked.

"Five thousand dollars. Six max," Felicia answered. "But we're really hoping you can do it for four." She flashed a hopeful smile that revealed a tiny gap in her front teeth.

On cue, Ashley and Mia stole a glance at each other. Five would barely cover their expenses, not to mention putting on the event.

Ashley's look clearly said, "It's your decision, but I like them."

"Why don't I have Ashley put some ideas together for you about what is feasible and we'll get back to you with a proposal by the end of the week. How's that?"

The sisters smiled in unison. The gap mirrored.

Felicia stuck out her hand toward Mia. "Thank you so much." She shook Mia's hand then did the same with Ashley.

"I really hope you consider taking us on," Linda said, the first time she'd spoken since they'd arrived.

Ashley stood, her notebook pressed against her small breasts. "By the way, I meant to ask, how did you find out about us?"

"Oh, a friend of ours who helped to get our business up and running," Felicia offered.

"Michael Burke," the sisters sang in harmony.

"He recommended you very highly," Felicia added.

Mia held back a yelp of surprise. Her pulse pounded so loudly that the voices faded into the background. She wasn't sure if she'd even said goodbye.

The sound of the front door closing snapped her to attention. She was alone in the conference room.

Recommended by Michael Burke. Coincidence or just her luck? Manhattan, for all its pomp and circumstance and worldwide notoriety, was nothing more than an island jam-packed with people and buildings. Sooner or later paths were bound to cross.

So he hadn't forgotten about her and even thought enough of her to recommend a possible client. She didn't know if it was a good or a bad thing, but it was the one thing, the opening that she needed.

They had nothing in common—
except red-hot desire!

National bestselling author

Marcia King-Gamble

TEMPTING
M O GUL
the

Life coach Kennedy Fitzgerald's assignment grooming unconventional, sexy Salim Washington to take over as TV studio head has become a little too pleasurable. For both of them. But shady motivations and drama threaten to stall this merger before the ink's even dry!

Coming the first week of December
wherever books are sold.

KIMANI™
ROMANCE

www.kimanipress.com   KPMKG0931208

Too close for comfort…

National bestselling author

Gwyneth Bolton

THE LAW
OF DESIRE

Book #3 in Hightower Honors

Detective Lawrence Hightower's stakeout is
compromised by a beautiful, suspicious stranger.
Minerva Jones needs his protection—but he's not
so sure he can trust her. Minerva is intensely
attracted to the sexy cop, but she's got secrets…
and trouble is closing in.

HIGHTOWER HONORS

FOUR BROTHERS ON A MISSION TO PROTECT, SERVE AND LOVE…

*Coming the first week of December
wherever books are sold.*

KIMANI
ROMANCE

www.kimanipress.com   KPGB0941208

Will she let her past decide her future?

NATIONAL BESTSELLING AUTHOR
Melanie Schuster

trust
IN
Me

Playboy Lucien Deveraux is ready to settle
down and be a one-woman man. Trouble is,
Nicole Argonne has no time for "pretty boys"—
especially the reformed-player type. If Lucien
wants her, he needs to prove himself…and
Nicole's not going to make it easy.

"A richly satisfying love story."
—*Romantic Times BOOKreviews* on *Let It Be Me*

*Coming the first week of December
wherever books are sold.*

KIMANI™
ROMANCE

www.kimanipress.com   KPMS0951208

REQUEST YOUR FREE BOOKS!

2 FREE NOVELS
PLUS 2 FREE GIFTS!

KIMANI™
ROMANCE

Love's ultimate destination!

YES! Please send me 2 FREE Kimani™ Romance novels and my 2 FREE gifts (gifts are worth about $10). After receiving them, if I don't wish to receive any more books, I can return the shipping statement marked "cancel." If I don't cancel, I will receive 4 brand-new novels every month and be billed just $4.69 per book in the U.S. or $5.24 per book in Canada, plus 25¢ shipping and handling per book and applicable taxes, if any*. That's a savings of over 20% off the cover price! I understand that accepting the 2 free books and gifts places me under no obligation to buy anything. I can always return a shipment and cancel at any time. Even if I never buy another book from Kimani Press, the two free books and gifts are mine to keep forever.

168 XDN EF2D   368 XDN EF3T

Name	(PLEASE PRINT)	

Address		Apt. #

City	State/Prov.	Zip/Postal Code

Signature (if under 18, a parent or guardian must sign)

Mail to **The Reader Service:**
IN U.S.A.: P.O. Box 1867, Buffalo, NY 14240-1867
IN CANADA: P.O. Box 609, Fort Erie, Ontario L2A 5X3

Not valid to current subscribers of Kimani Romance books.

Want to try two free books from another line?
Call 1-800-873-8635 or visit www.morefreebooks.com.

* Terms and prices subject to change without notice. N.Y. residents add applicable sales tax. Canadian residents will be charged applicable provincial taxes and GST. Offer not valid in Quebec. This offer is limited to one order per household. All orders subject to approval. Credit or debit balances in a customer's account(s) may be offset by any other outstanding balance owed by or to the customer. Please allow 4 to 6 weeks for delivery. Offer available while quantities last.

Your Privacy: Kimani Press is committed to protecting your privacy. Our Privacy Policy is available online at www.eHarlequin.com or upon request from the Reader Service. From time to time we make our lists of customers available to reputable third parties who may have a product or service of interest to you. If you would prefer we not share your name and address, please check here. ☐

One moment can change your life....

Seduced BY Moonlight

NATIONAL BESTSELLING AUTHOR

Janice Sims

When Harrison Payne sees an intriguing stranger basking in the night air at his Colorado resort, he's determined to get to know her much better. Discovering that Cherisse Washington is the mother of a promising young skier he's agreed to sponsor is a stroke of luck; learning Cherisse's ex is determined to get her back is an unwanted setback. But all's fair in love and war....

Coming the first wefi of December wherever books are sold.

ARABESQUE®

www.kimanipress.com

KPJS1121208

Love, honor and cherish...

•

i promise

NATIONAL BESTSELLING AUTHOR

ADRIANNE
byrd

Beautiful, brilliant Christian McKinley could set the
world afire. Instead, she dreams of returning to her
family's Texas ranch. But Malcolm Williams has other
plans for her, publicly proposing to Christian at the
social event of the year. So how can she tactfully turn
down a proposal from this gorgeous, well-connected,
obscenely rich suitor? By inadvertently falling in love
with his twin brother, Jordan!

"Byrd proves once again that she's a wonderful
storyteller."—*Romantic Times BOOKreviews*
on *The Beautiful Ones*

Coming the first wefi of December wherever books are sold.

ARABESQUE®
www.kimanipress.com

KPAB1151208